Five Can Keep

a

Secret

Sharon McGregor

Whimsical Publications, LLC

Florida

Five Can Keep a Secret is a work of fiction. Names, characters, and incidents are the products of the author's imagination and are either fictitious or are used fictitiously. Any resemblance to actual events or persons, living or dead, is entirely coincidental.

If you purchased this book without a cover, you should be aware that this book may have been stolen property and reported as "unsold and destroyed" to the publisher. In such case, neither the publisher nor the author has received payment for this "stripped book."

To purchase the authorized electronic edition of *Five Can Keep a Secret*, visit
www.whimsicalpublications.com

Cover art by Shyanne England
Editing by Brieanna Robertson

ISBN-13: 978-1-63495-004-6

Published by
Whimsical Publications, LLC
Florida

"Sophie's managed to stay on the wagon for quite a while this time," said Karen when the door had closed. "I hope she's finally shaken off her demons."

"We all have demons to shake," said Sally with uncharacteristic gloom. "Do they ever totally go away?"

"Well, I'm for another glass of wine," said Marci. "Any other imbibers ready for more?"

Everyone except Will held up an empty glass for a refill. He gave Marci a negative salute with his half full glass. "I'll have to open a new one," said Marci. "There's some red left here, but we need a new white."

"Let's sort out the sleeping arrangements," said Jennifer. "Then we can get rid of that pile of luggage." She motioned to the pile of assorted bags they had all dumped by the far wall of the living area. "Sally, you and Karen can take the far room. Marci and Sophie can have the room with the moose head and I'll take the little one with the single bed. Will, sorry, but you have to settle for the couch."

While Marci opened and poured the wine, the others moved their cases into their assigned rooms. No one thought to complain that Jennifer automatically assumed the single room. After all, it was her cottage. Will helped them move.

"I don't even have a toothbrush," he grumbled.

"Well, you're not borrowing mine," said Jennifer. "I have some mouthwash unopened. You can pour out some for yourself, but that's as far as I go." She disappeared into her room to get the bottle and handed it to him.

"I'm going down to check the water pipe where it comes in to the cottage. It had a bit of a leak earlier, but I think I got it bunged up." No one was listening to his statement, so Will set the bottle of mouthwash on the counter, grabbed his jacket, and headed for the cellar.

Karen went to the bathroom, and the others began to unpack their clothes. In Sophie's absence, Marci chose the bed closest to the door. There was a good draft coming in through the window and Marci liked a warm, cozy bed. She also took the two top drawers of the dresser. Sophie, except for her shoes, always traveled light when it came to wardrobe, so one drawer and the remaining hangers would be enough for her.

Sally unpacked on her own. She took one more try at her

cell phone to see if she could get reception. She'd really like to hear Mac's voice even for a moment. Now was her chance to be alone, with Karen taking her extended smoke break in the bathroom. She giggled and wondered if Jennifer would be sniffing as she passed the bathroom door. She flung her phone down in disgust. She wouldn't get a line out until they left here and made it out as far as the highway. She could try the land line, but didn't want to talk to Mac with everyone listening.

After they had all unpacked and returned to the living room, Will took the remaining case, assuming it must be Sophie's, into the moose-head room. "Sophie must be smoking half the pack to make up for lost time," he said. "Doesn't she feel the cold? She's going to be frostbitten if she doesn't come in."

"Go yell at her out the door. She must be done with her cigarette by now." All five of them stopped as though with a common thought. Jennifer repeated, more seriously now, "Will, go get Sophie." The others exchanged worried looks.

"She's been gone a long time," said Karen. "Do you think she could have wandered off looking for something, maybe out to her car? It's down the drive a ways. She might get lost in the snow."

Will was only out for a minute when he gave a sudden shout, muffled against the wind but still audible. Jennifer ran to the door, followed by the others. Will pushed the door open part way. "She fell," he said. "She must have hit her head on something. She's hurt pretty bad. Help me bring her in. Or at least hold the door. I can lift her myself."

They stood in the cold, waiting for Will. He came in, dangling Sophie over his shoulder in a fireman's lift and, kneeling beside the couch, he laid her out. They crowded around. "Sophie, Sophie!" Jennifer was closest to her head and slapped her face lightly, trying to get her to move. They could all see the large gash on her head and the blood seeping from it.

"She's not moving. I don't think she's breathing." Jennifer put her face close to Sophie's and then held her finger at Sophie's neck. "There's no pulse," she said, leaning back on her heels and looking at the others, horror-struck. "I think she's dead."

Dedicated to my son Gavin for his unfailing support in all my projects.

Chapter One

Jennifer

Jennifer swore at the weatherman. Could you never trust them? Obviously not, according to the snow swirling across the highway in front of her. She hoped the others had left early. Should she have reminded them to check their tires and carry chains just in case?

She frowned into the streaked white landscape in front of her silver Volvo and cursed again. Her kid-gloved hands gripped the steering wheel with tight control. She was beginning to feel a few prickles of discontent about the upcoming days. She had planned the reunion down to the last detail, she'd thought, but she'd ignored the weatherman. She should have remembered that, in this part of the country, there was often a sudden bitter storm after a quiet Christmas. This time even the weatherman got it wrong. She hoped everyone would arrive in time before the snow got worse. Every one of them would be driving and probably a few hours behind her.

She knew she'd have no worries about the cottage being ready. Will would see to that. Jennifer had never really liked Will, her only cousin to remain in their hometown area. Privately, she called him ferret-face and a few other uncomplimentary nicknames, but she had never found him difficult to control. He might protest sometimes at doing what she asked, but he'd never failed her. Most people didn't fail Jennifer.

All Will had to do was to get the generator going and the water works flowing again in the old lake cottage. She expected by the time she got there, the place would be warm, the refrigerator stocked, and the hot water tank ready for the shower she was looking forward to.

She nearly missed the sign that announced the turn toward the lake. The sign had faded over the years and no one seemed concerned enough to give it a facelift.

She skidded a little as she braked, and gave a quick glance in her rear view mirror to be sure no one had been tailgating her. Then she corrected and made the right turn. This road was still paved, but a little further along she would turn onto a narrow gravel road leading her to the old family cottage. It was in Jennifer's name now, willed to her after the death of her grandparents. The other cousins, Will and Dierdre, had been left the farm and the house in town. Will had kept the farm, renting it out while he tended to his hardware store, but Dierdre had sold the house like a shot and headed for sunnier climes, along with her grasping husband and her two annoying children.

The road wasn't difficult yet; most of the snow was blowing right across, but little sharp-pointed fingers were beginning to form along the shoulders.

Jennifer wished she'd been able to see Aaron again before she'd left. He'd seemed strangely antagonistic towards her getaway.

"Why now?" he'd asked the night she'd told him about her plans. "Why arrange a reunion in the boonies somewhere in the dead of winter?"

"But that's the best time, darling," she'd argued. "It's a sort of hiatus for everyone. The family Christmas 'dos' are all finished and we'll be back by New Year's Eve. It's only for three days and the perfect time. No one is busy at work. I don't understand your objection."

He'd stopped his arguments when he realized she was going ahead whether he approved or not. They had been together long enough for him to know it was useless to try to change her mind once it had been made up.

In spite of her determination, Jennifer felt the need to convince him. Ever since their engagement, Jennifer had felt herself trying not to be caught wrong-footed, an unusual situation for her.

In her darker moments, Jennifer thought it might have something to do with what she saw when she looked in the mirror these days. She was still attractive, she knew, and she'd learned at an early age how to best present herself, much in the way she'd learned how to stage a house for sale. But at forty-five, she was well aware the facade would soon start to crumble. She'd been married before, a short unsuccessful marriage, and since then, she'd limited her romantic life to a series of lovers who suited her for the moment.

Now she thought the time had come to make long range plans. Aaron was wealthy, successful, and not bad-looking. He was a perfect catch. Not only that, but every once in a while, Jennifer startled herself by a wave of affection that swept over her in his company. She wasn't sure she'd call it love, but if not, it was a healthy substitute. She looked forward to becoming Mrs. Aaron Somers. Nothing must come in the way of that—nothing. And this week, she was going to ensure it didn't.

As a result, trying to explain the reasons for her plan, she had tried to keep a whinging note out of her voice. "Every time we try to plan something in town, at least one of us gets interrupted by family or business. Out at the lake with no one else around for miles, we can relax and catch up. Like a retreat, really. I'm going to miss you, you know," she said, changing course and curling her arms around his neck, nuzzling him gently. "You know we have these reunions every couple of years and this seemed like a good time. Besides, I haven't told them yet about us. They are my oldest friends."

"I still think it would be easier to have it here—nice and simple."

"We're college friends, darling. We like to get close to our old playfields and this cottage is only a short drive away from the university. We used to go there sometimes in the summer and have great parties."

"In the summer, yes," he said grudgingly. "Well, let me know as soon as you get back. And watch those roads for winter driving conditions. Now go take your shower. I'll whip us up something wonderful for a snack. If your fridge has anything edible in it, that is." Jennifer had never been much of a cook, probably because she usually lived alone. It was so much easier to go out or take in.

She hadn't even scraps of Christmas leftovers in the fridge. Christmas had been at Aaron's home, with an introduction to his grown daughter, something Jennifer had not been looking forward to but which went surprisingly well.

Jennifer wasn't sure what had changed that night, but something had. When she came out of the shower, Aaron had a distant expression on his face. He had asked her a few questions about the friends she was going to meet and then left early, without their usual rematch. She put it down to holiday angst, but reflecting back, she wondered if he was upset she had made plans first and told him second. She had only seen him once more, briefly, before she left. She had the feeling then that he had looked at her as though waiting for the answer to a question she hadn't heard him ask.

Now she slowed, watching for familiar checkpoints to mark her turn. There was no other traffic on the side road, but it was still clear and quite drivable. When she came to the turn-off, she stopped the car and brought out from the back seat a bunch of colored balloons, which she tied to a hydro pole. Hopefully they would last till the rest of the girls arrived. She didn't know if they had GPS or if this road would even show up on it. She had never felt comfortable with GPS herself after being directed the wrong way onto a one-way street once. She had torn it off the dash and flung it into the dumpster in a fit of pique and never purchased another. She trusted her own sense of direction more. This seemed as good a way as any to mark the trail. Cell phone service here was spotty at best. It had been years since any of them had been here, but they should make this far at least by memory.

It was another mile to the cottage. She could just make out the lines of the old building and could see a trail of smoke coming from the roof. At least Will had a fire going. Hopefully, everything else was ready as well. She pulled in to the yard, far away from the entrance to allow the others room to park. No sign of Will's vehicle, so hopefully he had completed his chores. She didn't want him around when the girls arrived. Girls—what a strange way to refer to a group of forty-something women, but girls they would always be, friends from school trapped in a teenage warp of friendship.

She unloaded the car, bringing one suitcase and a bag with a few goodies in it she hadn't trusted Will to find. His taste in wine was a bit lacking, not to mention the atrocity he would choose in the name of Scotch.

She dropped her bag by the large black leather sofa in the main room and set about checking her supplies. The fridge was humming and the cottage was still cool but should be warm soon with the electric heater and the wood fireplace going. The generator was working properly. She went to the bathroom and turned the tap. Nothing. What had Will done, gallop off without making sure they had water? But, of course, he hadn't galloped off. She looked out the living room window and spotted his truck, parked at the back of the cottage.

The door creaked open and she heard her cousin's familiar voice. "Sorry, I had a glitch with the water pipes. It won't take long to get it going."

"I hope not. Everyone will be here soon and I'd like a shower before they do."

"You might have to wait on the shower. Even when I get the water flowing through the pipes again, you'll have to wait for the hot water tank to heat it up."

"Lovely," said Jennifer with as much sarcasm as she could squeeze into one word.

Will paid no attention. He was too used to her. "I'll get some more firewood," he said. "I used it all up just getting the fire going. I hope that axe is still in the cellar. You don't want to run out. And then I'll finish with the water. I'd better move my truck around front too, before your crowd blocks me in."

A few minutes later, Jennifer heard a car pull into the driveway. She knew which one of her friends it would be without even looking. Sally, the one who always felt she had to put in the extra effort to please, always the first to volunteer for the dirty jobs, always the first to arrive, always the first to agree to everything Jennifer suggested.

She smiled at that thought. Having a quick agreement from one of her group had always made it easier to convince the others. She almost considered waylaying Sally before the others arrived to tell her why she wanted them here, but that might complicate things. Better to face them all together. Besides, she needed to warm them up with a few memories first. And then there was Will. She wished he'd finish and leave.

She took a lingering look at the sparkling ring on her left hand and removed it, thrusting it into her front pocket. Time for announcements later. She wanted to do things on her selected time line.

Fixing her welcome on her face, she went to greet Sally at the door.

Chapter Two

Sally

Sally snuck another glance at the speedometer. Her foot was getting a little heavy and she adjusted accordingly. She was normally a cautious driver—overcautious, her husband Mac said—but she was anxious to get to the cottage before the snow got worse, and her foot on the accelerator seemed to have a short cut mapped to her fears. She wished she was back home. She wished she hadn't agreed to come to the stupid reunion. She let out a long sigh, knowing that last one was impossible. When had she ever been able to say no to Jennifer? When had any of them for that matter? It was just that Sally had always been the first to capitulate. The weakest, she told herself with a sneer.

She wished she knew why Jennifer had arranged the reunion for now. They generally had them every two or three years, but it had been less than two since their last one. There was usually a reason behind the timing. The previous one had been just after Jennifer had received a Woman of Distinction award right on the heels of her Real Estate Salesperson of the Year trophy. At least that one hadn't been littered with the landmines some of the get-togethers were. You never knew just where Jennifer was headed sometimes with her conversations. You merely feared the worst and breathed a sigh of relief to know you weren't the intended recipient of her veiled comments. She wondered how the others felt about these reunions. Were they all as nervous as she was, or did they laugh it all off and just enjoy the reminiscing? Maybe they didn't have secrets to hide the way she did. No, she was pretty sure each one of them had something in their past that Jennifer knew and trotted out occasionally in cryptic comments designed to be understood only by one person, but also intended to let her know who had the knowledge, who had the power.

But then, maybe Sally, as usual, was exaggerating. After all, Jennifer, as far as she knew, had never passed on any secret knowledge regarding any of them, never betrayed her friends, and never done anything to justify the deep dread Sally always felt in her presence.

Mac knew how worked up she got every time a party was arranged and responded with his ever practical, "Just don't go."

"I have to go," she said. "It's been two years since I've seen them and it would be unsociable, not to mention cowardly, if I didn't."

"You have to learn to ignore Jennifer," he chided. "I know she gets up your nose. She gets up mine too, even if I only saw her twice, but she's not important to you. She's not important to us." Seeing she was still dithering, Mac went on, "Would you like us to pray together?"

"No!" said Sally, realizing immediately that she had spoken too forcefully. It was not the response expected from a pastor's wife.

It was strange that, of the five of them, two had married ministers. Thanks heavens she got the best of the deal there, thought Sally. Mac was a country preacher. He loved his vocation, loved his wife, and loved his God. He met everyone with an expectation of their inner goodness and he even managed to accept the times the goodness failed to materialize. Why then did Sally not have faith in his ability to forgive her if he knew the truth?

She thought of Karen then and wondered how she managed to keep her calm in a marriage to Kenneth. He was a minister too, in a large city parish with a good-sized congregation. Kenneth and Mac were so different they might be from two unrelated species.

When they were students, they would have described Kenneth as a man who walked around with a broomstick up his butt. She giggled at the thought and wondered again how Karen came to marry him and why she stuck it out. She thought she knew the answer to the second one. Security.

Not usually the word you'd associate with a man in the ministry, but Karen had been left a widow with two children by a man who had gambled and invested badly with all their money. Kenneth must have looked like a beacon of sanity to her. Unfortunately, from what Sally knew of him, he was also controlling, judgmental, and had a vicious temper. What a strange choice of profession. But then his congregation was right-wing and, to her view, a fanatical group of people, and he and his flock must have a need for each other.

Sally didn't see the turn-off sign until she was almost beside it. She pulled to the shoulder and waited till a semi flew by spewing chunks of snow at her, then reversed and pulled into the secondary road.

It was a little scarier driving in the snow with no painted highway lines to guide her, but she was used to country roads and could still remember some of the terrain from her visits years ago, the two little dips, a winding right turn, and then she spotted the balloons. Now she would be there in a few minutes.

She almost uttered a prayer seeking help to guide her through the next few days, but the words stuck in her throat the way her disbelief lodged in her heart. How could she believe in a God who would let terrible things happen? A God who would take away everything she wanted in life just because of a few minutes of stolen pleasure. Pleasure! She nearly choked on the words. There had been no pleasure. Her eyes misted over and she took one hand from the steering wheel to wipe the tears away. The road was already drifting over and she didn't want to go in the ditch.

Two vehicles stood in the yard. She thought the Volvo must be Jennifer's. Last time they had met, that's what Jennifer had driven—a different one, of course. The other vehicle was a truck with a sort of camper cab. She couldn't match that choice to any of the girls. Then she saw a man carrying a load of firewood from the small shed in the rear. Will. She remembered him and gave a wave as he looked in her direction and smiled.

He disappeared inside with the armload of wood. Sally pulled behind the Volvo. Best not to block the truck, as she imagined Will would be leaving as soon as he had everything done according to Jennifer's satisfaction.

She gritted her teeth, opened her car door, and pulled out her small case from the back seat. *Three days*, she thought. *Three days and three nights. Surely I can get through that.* She hoped the others would show up soon. She didn't relish time alone with Jennifer. Maybe Will would stay, aborting any awkward conversations. She shivered. Why had she used that word?

Chapter Three

Marci

Marci flew along the highway, CD blasting out classic rock, singing along at the top of her lungs. She knew she was getting close to the turn-off and slowed just in time to see the billboard announcing the lake road. As she turned, the Jerry Lee Lewis CD ended and she didn't replace it with another. She needed to concentrate on getting her bearings. The car fell eerily silent.

She had almost not come this time. The heck with Jennifer and her sad attempts to corral them on a regular basis to confirm her place at the head of the pecking order. Marci could live without that quite nicely, thanks. Still, the girls were a part of her past, an important part, and she had known all along she would come, no matter how much she protested for the past two days.

Dena had encouraged her, nearly pushing her out the door. "You'll never know what you missed if you miss it," she said with a weird twist of logic. Seeing Marci's exaggerated eyebrow raise, she went on. "You know what I mean. If you don't go, you won't accomplish anything anyhow. Your mind will be with them the whole time. Besides, I'm not going to be here either. Time for my annual bonding with Sister Ellen." Dena's sister was a real sister, a nun, and she usually visited her family only once a year. In spite of her qualms about Dena's lifestyle, Marci knew they were still close.

Marci's expression softened at the thought of Dena as she had left her, half curled around a pillow, blonde hair fanned out above her head, covers in a tangle, a glistening afterglow on her golden skin. She felt the usual tug at the core of her being that came every time she thought of Dena. Nearly five years together and she never tired of the intricate and exquisite variety of her. Maybe it was time to put things on a more permanent footing. They often talked about the future—about plans for holidays next year, or about some adventure they might share. But never had the idea of marriage come up. Marci wasn't sure why. All their friends knew about their relationship. Dena's family had met her. Marci had no family left to consult.

Marci felt a need to formalize their relationship, a seeking for security, maybe. She'd hinted once or twice, but Dena had never taken the bait. Had she deliberately ignored the allusions or had she truly not known where Marci's conversation had been headed? She was afraid to push, afraid of a rebuff. Once the box was opened, it could never be closed again. She was afraid to risk a relationship already perfect by trying to make it more so.

Sometimes, in her happiest daydreams, she pictured presenting Dena with a ring, on bended knee if necessary. Would her face mirror happiness or shock?

She jerked the wheel around a huge snow finger on the side of the road. Damn Jennifer and her timing. She nearly slid into the ditch there. She looked around and saw no sign of life—no other cars on the road, not even lights against the growing twilight. She was happy to make it before dark. This road would be a killer when you couldn't see at all, and the snow was driving directly into her windshield now, nearly hypnotizing her.

The turn should be close. She spotted the balloons and slowed nearly to a stop as she took the corner onto the last mile of road to the cottage. She saw a mound beside the road as she turned—a car, she saw, hopefully not one of theirs. She stopped carefully, afraid to brake too hard and slide down the bank into the snow the way this car apparently had. It hadn't been there long. Not a lot of snow had accumulated.

She got out of her car, leaving the door open, and walked close enough to make out that no one was inside the ditched one. It was abandoned, the owner probably safe in a warm house waiting for a tow truck to come the next day. She didn't see any footprints around the vehicle, but then the swirling snow would cover them nearly as soon as they were made. Feeling she had done her duty as far as needed, she slid back into her car and started forward again. The rear end swung round and she braced herself for a slide, but mercifully, the car straightened itself and slowly moved forward, spinning snow behind the tires until it set a straight course along the snow-rutted lane.

She should have stayed home, she thought again. Even if Dena was away, especially if Dena was away, it would give her time to catch up on some work. Marci had never climbed to the heights she had expected in her career after college. She went on to get her masters in marine biology, but had dawdled around putting off her doctorate, delaying the inevitable messages she knew would come from Jennifer when she started to publish. She grinned. Funny, really. After years of anticipating Jennifer's response to her academic papers, she had gone a different route, writing a textbook aimed at younger grades.

She finally figured the best way around Jennifer was to confront her directly and tell her what she planned. It had been amazingly easy, but then, at the time, Jennifer had other fish to fry. Now with three more books under her belt, she had begun work on her doctorate research. A little late, but better than never. With her research, her mainstream books, and her work at the aquarium, she had a busy life. She always thought of it as a happy life. The only times she had doubts was when faced with one of these blasted reunions.

She looked away from the lane only briefly, caught by a flash in her rear view mirror. A car was close behind her. So she wasn't the last to arrive. She wondered which one was trailing her. Someone who drove faster than she did, apparently, because she had seen no one behind her a few minutes ago. Or had the lights been shrouded by the snow? She'd only stopped a minute to check the abandoned car.

She pulled into the yard, parking as close to the door as she could. The driver of the second car swung in to park behind her. No need to worry about blocking another vehicle now. They were here for the duration. She counted vehicles. Five. So they were all here. But which one had taken to driving a truck?

She unloaded her car, pulling out a heavy duffel bag, which she swung onto the snow, pausing to wave hello in the direction of the dark green SUV that had followed her into the yard.

Chapter Four

Karen

Karen enjoyed driving, at least when she was alone. She loved the little cocoon she made for herself on these occasions, solitary and excluding. Her life existed on the other side of the metal box, not within. Sometimes she would let her imagination take her to freedom. What would happen if she just kept driving? Drove and drove for days, only stopping for gas and food. How many days would it take to put Kenneth behind her?

She gave a little shudder. In her darker moments, she knew she'd never be able to put Kenneth behind her. Her savior had become her captor.

There were days when she couldn't remember what it had been like BK—Before Kenneth. It was as if she had been born again—she nearly giggled at that thought, how apt—on the day she married Kenneth.

Life hadn't been easy BK, but it had felt real. She had felt real, with all the worry and uncertainty life had a way of dealing you along with the good. The good had been short. Eight years with

Terry. Eight years of relative harmony and a good dollop of love. She didn't let herself think of those years too often. It was easy to get lost in them, and the pain was a physical torment when she returned to the present.

Eight years with Terry and then she had been left with two young girls and the empty half of a king-sized bed. A drunk driver with a need for speed, and Terry in the wrong place. Widowhood had settled on her in a blanket of grief for a long time before she realized the girls were as bereft as she was.

Terry had been a wonderful husband and father, but not a good money manager. His hopes for the future of his family exceeded his ability to fulfill them. He made bad business deals with the optimism of a confirmed gambler. Nothing ever worked out for them. The house didn't have enough equity to merit a second mortgage to pay the bills. She sold it, but what was left didn't go far, not with two young girls who needed a future. Brielle and Melody needed all the accoutrements she couldn't afford. They needed figure skating lessons and costumes and road trips and dance lessons—the list went on.

Karen found a half-decent job, but it wouldn't make a dent in providing for their future. There would be college ahead, and training for good careers, to send them into the world confident and armed.

Enter Kenneth. Karen went to a local church one Sunday with a girl from work who had been especially nice to her, and she couldn't think of a way to decline the offer. She wasn't normally a church-goer, but Cora-lee had insisted she'd find comfort there. She had introduced her to the minister afterwards, and Kenneth Gordon had taken her under his wing. He'd been a comforter, a shoulder for her, and a support. Brielle hadn't liked him from the start, but Melody had fallen to his charm. And so had Karen.

Two months later, he proposed. It took her by surprise with its suddenness, but Kenneth had honeyed the proposal with plans for the girls, with talks of the colleges they could send them to, with hope for a future. Karen was pretty sure she had never loved Kenneth, even when she accepted the proposal, but she had been swept along by the vision he painted for her of their life ahead. She hadn't even stopped to question where a small city preacher would find the money for his plans. She had reached gratefully for the life vest he held out. She heard him talk of well-to-do family, but strangely, none of them were able to attend their wedding. Yet, he always seemed to have money, so perhaps he had an inheritance somewhere to supplement his stipend from the church. Money matters were not discussed with Karen, even now.

It wasn't long before Kenneth began to mold her into the shape of the wife he wanted. It began with subtlety and she quickly modified her behavior in a wish to please her new husband. The manipulation became more advanced and more open, but in such a slow process she never noticed the change until one day she realized she had no friends of her own and she and the girls spent their days walking on eggshells to please Kenneth.

She tried to tell Kenneth how she felt, but his anger, although never physical, was a frightening thing to behold. He seemed to know her soft spots, how to hurt her in many small ways, how to threaten without threatening. He was so accomplished at this he could do it with others present, and all anyone else thought was how wonderful their minister had been to offer such a good home to a widow with two girls.

Karen had no money of her own and no access to Kenneth's income. He had convinced her to stop work and become a "proper wife" shortly after their wedding. He wasn't miserly, just controlling. The credit cards were in his name and he monitored her shopping allowance and household expenditures. It became a Saturday tradition. Armed with receipts and bills, she would list for him everything she had bought during the week. The girls had their designer clothing and their lessons, but they knew who was responsible for their perfect lives. They were reminded every day.

Karen's bank account had just over forty dollars in it. She had no family of her own. An only child of unlucky parents who both died of cancer. No one was left to tell her if she was really being manipulated by a master of the art or if she was merely an ungrateful wife. She began to fantasize. She imagined what it would be like if Kenneth were to be hit by a misfortune someday. Maybe a car accident or a robbery gone wrong, or... She knew she had to pull herself out of those thoughts. They could lead to danger.

She could just walk away, of course. There were no bars on her prison. She could take Melody—Brielle was already in her second year of college—and walk out the door with only her personal possessions. But where would she go? In an uncertain economic climate, would she even find a job? Would her daughters ever forgive her for pulling them out of school and plunging them into poverty?

She only needed to last another four years. Melody would enter university in the autumn and Brielle had two years to go. Then they would be independent and she would be free.

This was the stuff of her daydreams.

Once, earlier on, she had planned her escape, prepared to sacrifice everything for a new life away from Kenneth. She began to squirrel away money from her housekeeping allowance and opened a secret bank account. When she had enough, she could make her escape to another city and another home. She was only up to three hundred dollars when Kenneth discovered her secret. That's when the Saturday accountings had begun.

Karen wondered why Kenneth didn't stop her from attending the reunion with her old friends. Maybe he didn't see them as a threat, coming into her life only once every few years. Maybe he knew she looked forward to them with dread instead of pleasure.

Maybe she was paranoid. Could she possibly be misinterpreting the things he did and said? No. Because Brielle and Melody had come to the same conclusion she had. They both urged her to leave, to not mind about their college years. They would get by. And they would too—get by, that is. The problem was she wanted more for them than to just get by. And she was so conditioned now to her way of interacting with Kenneth she didn't know if she was capable of escaping. Sometimes she wished he would hit her. That would be easy. She could flee home with the support of a whole community of helpers. She would have bruises that showed on the outside.

His last words to her were, "Have fun with your friends." How could you convince people this was a man who liked to bully and torment?

She swung off the main highway with a wild swerve, nearly hitting the ditch in a fishtail before the car straightened. The little frisson of fear she felt was almost pleasant, like an emotional orgasm.

She was still driving too fast, she knew. She thought she could just make out a red glow of taillights ahead. One of the other girls? So she wasn't the only late-comer. The driver in front slowed to turn down the last lane, but stopped on the corner. Only for a moment, then she went on. As Karen followed, she saw the reason for the pause. A vehicle in the ditch was steadily accumulating a snow cover. Obviously no one was in distress or the other car would have stopped, so Karen went on. She was right on the heels of the other vehicle and slowed a little to avoid tailgating. She pulled into the yard close behind. She pulled out her keys and stood up slowly, taking the kinks out of her back and legs. She acknowledged the cheery wave from the other driver with an answering one, counting the vehicles. "Hi, Marci. Looks like we're all here?"

Chapter Five

Sophie

Damn the snow! Sophie shouted out loud to the silent car and banged the steering wheel in frustration. She hated driving in snow. Not only were the lines on the highway nearly obscured, but the wind was blowing the flakes directly at her windshield, making an almost hypnotic picture. She struggled to keep her eyes on the road. She could do with a cigarette now, but she was afraid to take her attention from her driving long enough to fish one out and light it.

A semi pulled up behind her and she had the additional problem of his lights flashing in her mirrors. She was likely driving much too slowly for him if he'd caught her so suddenly. She slowed a bit more and tried to pull over to the right. She wanted him to pass but was afraid to go too far and slide off the shoulder. The driver's impatience must have won out over his caution and he swung off to the left, passing her in a cloud of whirling snow. For a second, she couldn't see, panicking into braking. A total white wall in front of her cleared slightly and she let her foot off the brake. She was nearly at a standstill. Luckily she hadn't hit a slippery spot and fishtailed when she braked.

She increased her speed slowly, glad of the semi's lights in front of her, a beacon showing her the center of the road. She hadn't met anyone in ages. It was as though she and the semi were the only fools left on a snow-filled highway. Soon she gave up trying to follow. She felt uncomfortable with his speed. She slowed even more, straining to see the turn-off. She knew it should be close.

It was. The old sign was barely visible, but she made the

turn. Only a few more miles on this road to the final turn. She wished she'd left home earlier. Or better still, decided against coming at all. Where Jennifer was concerned, that wasn't an option, though. She often wondered if it was only her that felt like an insect on a dissecting pin when Jennifer made her pointed comments. When they were in college, she hadn't paid much attention. Let's face it, she hadn't paid much attention to anything then except trying to clear her hangovers in the morning before first class. Sophie was now one husband, two jobs, and ten years past her last drink. She intended to stay that way. She wished she could do the same with cigarettes, but thought she deserved one crutch.

The wipers were now tracing gobs of snow back and forth across the windshield. Sophie could see no lights before her or behind her. She had to stop and clear the snow. She slowly eased her foot on the brake, hoping not to find a sheet of ice underneath. She half stood in the car doorway and pushed the snow from the driver's side wiper, then stood shakily to move towards the front of the car. The headlights were covered in a glaze of snow and ice. No wonder she couldn't see past her face. She cleared the glass and slid back into the car, already ten degrees colder. She held her breath a moment before inching forward. Success! She still couldn't see more than a few feet ahead, but at least now she could make out thicker snow lines along the side of the road where a plough had cleared some earlier snowfall. It gave her something to gauge where the ditch might be. She should have taken advantage of her stop to light a cigarette, but she wasn't going to risk another one.

At least the next three days would take some of the chill out of the empty house she had over the holidays. Jeff had given her the heave-ho a week before Christmas. What kind of a rat dumps his girlfriend the week before Christmas? She was probably better off without him, but one person rattling around in a three-bedroom old house with no company but a cat stretched her serenity to the limit. Bianca, her tortoise-shell, hadn't been happy to be shipped off to the neighbor's. Sophie could have gone to her sister's for Christmas. Andrea had asked her. Somehow, the thought of Andrea's white picket fence perfection with her two high-achieving progeny and her oh so successful husband wasn't the solution. It would only underline all the things missing in Sophie's own life. She knew it was terrible of her to think that way. Andrea loved her and had supported her even in her darkest years. She really did love her niece and nephew, and Jon wasn't that bad either. Maybe next year she'd spend the holidays with Andrea—next year when she had her life sorted out again.

She was nearly crawling now. The last tracks to take this road were nearly filled in, odd blank patches showing from time to time, but few clues to tell her she was still on the road. She could barely see the old piles of snow at the edges. When she finally made it to the corner, she breathed in a huge sigh of relief.

She made the turn and spotted the top of a car to her right. For one crazed moment, she thought she'd missed the road. Then she realized the nearly hidden car was in the ditch and resolved not to follow it in. Less than a mile to go. She squinted into the night, barely able to see the road. Only the slightly-raised mounds of snow along the side indicated where the edge of the road was, and they were barely visible. She limped along until she hit a large snowbank overflowing the road and the car stopped. She gunned the accelerator and the tires spun, not moving her car one bit. She pushed her door open, holding it against the growing wind, and surveyed the scene. It didn't look that bad, she thought. Maybe it was just an icy patch under her tires. She fumbled in the trunk for the shovel she had thought to include, as well as a couple of patches of carpet.

She scraped away in front of her tires with the shovel. Her face stung in the bitter wind and the snow slipped under her ridiculously high-heeled boots, but she persisted until the shovel began to spit gravel. When it looked as good as she was probably going to get it, she shoved the two bits of carpet under the tires and climbed back in, stepping on the gas. The car lurched and started to move. Success! She didn't stop to pick up the pieces of carpet, afraid she'd lose her momentum. She celebrated too soon. A few minutes later, the car swerved to the side again, all on its own. She tried to correct, but seemed to only make things worse. It dug into the rising bank on the side of the road, the rear end in the ditch, the front sideways across the track. She got out of the car and assessed the damage. Nothing was going to shift it now.

Ahead of her, she could see a faint glow of light. She knew she must be nearly at the cottage as the blowing snow would obscure anything farther than a few yards away. She turned off the lights and the engine, grabbed her small case and purse, and stomped off through the snow, her eyes fixed firmly on the yellow glow.

The wind was sharp through the hooded jacket she pulled close round her face; she felt cold to the bone in the few minutes it took her to reach the cottage door.

She fumbled with the handle for a minute with numbing fingers when it was thrown wide open by someone from the inside.

"Sophie! We'd given up on you."

Chapter Six

The Cottage

Sophie shed the few belongings she was carrying and made a beeline for the warmth of the fireplace, just stopping to take in the gathering on the way.

She looked at Jennifer with a scowl and said, "Tell me again why you thought it was a good idea to have a reunion in the middle of a snowstorm with no living creatures but us around for miles."

Jennifer shrugged and smiled, maddeningly pleasant. "We're all here safe and sound, aren't we?" Then she turned to the sole man in the room, the one who'd flung the door open in front of Sophie. "So everything is working now?"

"All set to go, I'm on my way home. You're going to be snowbound for a couple of days. No one is going anywhere till this ends and the ploughs come out, and that's not going to be soon. This lane isn't on their list, so I'll likely have to come with a tractor and blade to dig you out. Oh, and I left your tap dripping a bit. Don't turn it off. That might just be enough to keep the pipes from freezing until this old place warms up a little more."

Sophie remembered the man now—Will, Jennifer's cousin and gopher. He sometimes joined them on their party forays, but Sophie remembered him as a bit of a party-pooper. Of course, in those days, she thought of everyone that way, when she thought of them at all. "I'm sorry, Will, but that not going anywhere is going to include you too. You're not getting out of here."

"Oh, I'll make it. If you just got in, I'm sure I'll get out with the four-by-four. I have to go now, though." He looked at Jennifer. "You're welcome," he said to her unspoken and probably un-thought thanks.

"You don't understand," said Sophie. "I have no doubts on your driving abilities or your vehicle. It's just that I've blocked the road—completely. Just a few yards out. I couldn't make the last little bit. There's no way you can get around me."

"Give me your keys," he said. "I'll see if I can shift your car."

She handed them to him, knowing full well he'd never budge it. Jennifer frowned at him. "Why did you drive over? Don't you have a snowmobile? You could have used that and there'd be no problem getting out." Her voice held more than a trace of petulance.

"Sorry, princess. First, I didn't know I was going to have to hang around this long getting everything to your royal satisfaction. Second, the forecast never predicted this. Third, how was I to know one of your lot was going to drive like a woman and block my way?"

Sophie jumped to retort at the "drive like a woman," but subsided quickly as Will was already out the door and, besides, she was a woman. How else was she supposed to drive?

She fumbled in her purse and opened her pack of cigarettes, shaking one out in her hand.

"Not inside," said Jennifer in her no-nonsense voice.

"Oh come on. It's freezing out there. I'm still shaking from the cold and I need a smoke."

"Sorry, but this is a no-smoke cottage and you're the only one of us who indulges, so I repeat, 'Not inside'."

Sophie looked around at the others who either looked away or shrugged. She was pretty sure they wouldn't mind, but Jennifer was the only one with a vote. She popped the cigarette back in the pack and held her hands out to the fire.

Karen gave her a smile of conspiracy, slipping out a pack of cigarettes from her purse to show Sophie. She whispered, "We'll go out together later."

Jennifer swung round and said, "You too, Karen? I thought you gave them up ages ago. Well, you're still outvoted. There are four non-smokers and two smokers here, so we win."

Sophie shrugged. She'd wait till she got warm first and

slip outside the front door. The no-smoke cottage was a total fabrication on Jennifer's part. Sophie could remember a lot of smoking going on here in the long-ago and not all of it was cigarettes. Jennifer herself smoked back in the misty past.

The door opened, bringing in a swirl of snow and cold and a cross-looking Will.

"How did you manage to get it stuck like that?"

"Is that frustration speaking or do you really want an answer to a stupid question?" asked Sophie. "I got stuck because, if you didn't notice, there's a howling blizzard out there and I couldn't see more than two feet in front of the car."

"Sorry. It doesn't matter anyhow." Will backed down a little, his face still tight in disapproval. "It's so thick white out there now I couldn't make it to the road anyhow. I don't know how you got as far as you did. Why did you pick this week of all times to come to a remote cottage? There's nowhere in the city you could have done this?"

"Old history, Will. And the purpose of a retreat is to get away from it all."

"That's what this is—a retreat? I thought it was a girly gab-fest and a chance to get snookered without having to face down a breathalyser."

Jennifer ignored the comment. "So how are you going to get home, Will? Can you walk?"

He gave her a mutinous look. "I came here out of the goodness of my heart and got your generator going and your water on for your stupid reunion. With not a lot of thanks, I might add. And now you expect me to walk home when I can't see past my feet? I'm not going to freeze to death in a heap twenty feet from the door. No, I'm afraid you're stuck with me till this is over."

Jennifer sucked in a breath, but no words came out. She must have realized it was a losing battle. Sophie found amusement in the fact that Jennifer was in a situation she couldn't control.

The four sat on the two huge couches, Sophie and Sally on the one, Marci and Karen the other, eyes turned to watch the match between Will and Jennifer. *Someone should be selling tickets,* thought Sophie.

The show was a non-starter. Jennifer forced her mouth into a smile.

"Sorry, Will. Of course you can't leave in this weather. We'll just have to make do till the morning. Then when the snow and wind die down, you can walk across the fields to get home. You should be able to get away by then."

"You're all heart." He made a survey of the others. "Does anyone have a cell phone that works? Mine isn't getting a signal." He patted his pocket. "It never does work well here, but today it's totally dead."

They all fished out their phones and one by one looked up at him with the bad news. "Sorry, no service."

Sophie picked up the land-line and said, "Nothing there either. Who would you call anyway? No one would be able to come and get you. Even if they had a snowmobile, they'd get lost in the white-out."

"I wasn't looking for a ride home. I need to call someone to look after Buster. He's alone in the house."

"Your dog?"

"No, my cat." He seemed startled when Sophie and Marci both giggled.

"What's wrong with a cat?" Will demanded.

"Nothing, nothing," said Sophie, still chuckling. "You just don't look like a cat owner. I pictured Buster as a black lab off hunting with you or walking the back forty."

"I don't have a back forty. I'm not a farmer. I have a hardware store. Which is going to be closed tomorrow. I'm going to be losing business."

"What sort of business would you normally get in a blizzard in the middle of the holidays?"

"Not much," Will admitted sheepishly. "Sorry. I'm just upset to be stuck here when I could be doing something constructive. Buster has a litter box and food and water, so he'll survive. I guess we all have to suck it up and make the best of it. Now what's for supper?"

Jennifer was the first to move. "I think we stick with the simple tonight," she said. "There's a frozen lasagna big enough for us all and lots of stuff for a salad." She pulled the lasagna out of a bag on the table. It hadn't made it to the freezer yet. Most of the groceries were still on the counter. Sally jumped up to start putting things away in the small fridge and the cupboards.

Marci came over to help and Sophie threw away the

thought of a badly needed cigarette and started to slice veg-
etables for the salad.

Karen pulled a bottle from the door ledge in the fridge.
"White okay, or do we have to have red?"

"There's both," said Jennifer. "Red is on top of the fridge.
Might as well open one of each." She pulled out six glasses.
"How about you, Sophie? What are you drinking?"

"Anything not designed to raise the fun level," she said.
"Do you have cola?"

"In the fridge. Help yourself."

Sally moved aside to let Sophie's hand hover over the cola before grabbing a flavored sparkling water, and finished
putting the rest of the things away.

She took one of the glasses and nearly filled it to the
overflowing point with white wine. Sophie gave her a quick
glance. It seemed unlike Sally, but she shrugged. Who was
she to judge, and maybe Sally needed to kick off the traces
of being a pastor's wife occasionally. Besides, none of Mac's
parishioners would see her if she decided to get plastered
anyhow.

Chapter Seven

Sophie
25 years earlier

The fire burned high in the pit. Smoke swirled this way and that in the darkness, causing the watchers to shift out of its reach. A ghetto blaster was loud enough to cover the crackle of the flames, but the conversation was raised booze-level above the music.

Sophie took a long last pull on her cigarette and threw the butt into the fire. She choked on the smoke and drowned the raspy cough with a swill of beer. She chugalugged the last of the can and crumpled it in the center, reaching around Kevin to search for another. He pulled her closer till her head rested on his shoulder and said in a loud whisper into her ear, "Let's go have some fun."

Sophie let him pull her into a standing position, but made sure to stuff another can of beer into her jacket pocket. No one seemed to care or notice them leave the group. The others were all occupied with their own pursuits, dancing close to the fire, in lusty grasps on and under blankets, singing along with the music. Sophie could see Jennifer in a clinch with Rod, her current boyfriend. Jennifer gave her a wink over Rod's shoulder, but she was the only one to watch them go.

Kevin pulled her out of sight of the campfire and dangled a set of car keys in front of her. "Whose?" she asked, since she and Kevin had hitched a ride here with someone else.

"Tory's. He'll never notice. He's knee-deep into Trish at the moment and wouldn't notice an earthquake."

"He might be looking for the backseat of his car," said

Sophie.

"Naw, they have a sleeping bag. Come on. Let's do some fancy driving."

Kevin started the car and Sophie took the passenger seat. They drove a few hundred yards to the old gravel pit, where paths had been cut through the area for dirt bikes, mountain bikes, and hot-rodders.

"You first." He handed the keys to Sophie and she changed seats. She goosed the accelerator and raced though the dips, bouncing off the seat as the car took on air. This was fun. She reluctantly handed the keys back to Kevin, who took his turn at the dips. She cringed a little as one particular bounce shook the car. Tory wasn't going to be happy with them if they screwed his suspension.

"We'd better get the car back before we do damage or Tory sees we've gone," she said when Kevin came to a screeching stop beside her.

"See that break over there?" He pointed to a split in the wall that was sometimes used by bikers to jump across. "I bet I could make that in the car."

Sophie laughed. "You'd never make the jump. You'd crash into the pit below."

He merely grinned at her. "Wanna bet?"

"Never in a million years." Sophie, at this point, thought he was just kidding, that he wanted her to insist he not do it. Then he'd back down because she made him, not because of lack of machismo. But she didn't know Kevin as well as she thought. With a quick wave, he gunned the car and headed for the cliff.

Sophie called after him, "Wait, Kevin, no!" But she didn't yell loudly enough for him to hear her, and when she tried to move to stop him, her feet remained where they were. She felt a coldness sweep through her. She knew already this was not going to end well. Yet she watched the impending disaster as though it was on a screen and she was in the audience unable to affect the outcome, knowing it wasn't real.

He revved the car till the end swung out and released it, heading for the cut. The car left the edge and seemed to suspend there for a moment before nosing down the side, heading for the bottom. She heard the crash and began to scream, "Kevin!" but the sound remained within. She couldn't hear her voice.

Then she heard other voices. Dark shapes loomed out from the bushes, and beside her, Jennifer materialized, holding her by the shoulders.

"Wait," said Jennifer. "Let someone else go." She pulled Sophie in the other direction and sat her down on a boulder. Reaching for the beer in Sophie's pocket, she popped the snap and handed it to her. Sophie dutifully drank deeply from the can.

"I need to see how Kevin is," she said, standing up.

"No," said Jennifer. "You can't help him and someone else has already called for the ambulance. The best thing you can do is make as though you came out with the rest of us when you heard the crash."

"But why? I didn't do anything to get into trouble for."

"You took a car without permission and went joyriding. They could charge you, and if Kevin doesn't make it, the charges could get bad, even if you weren't in the car. Just trust me and do as I say."

Sophie pulled her jacket tightly around her shoulders and took another swig of the beer, allowing Jennifer to steer her. Isn't that what they always did—let Jennifer make the rules?

"Now throw your beer can into the trees," said Jennifer. Sophie finished it and complied. Everyone else in the group was doing the same.

It didn't take the sirens long to start. Sophie watched as they brought the stretcher up from the pit. She could see Kevin's head, uncovered. Surely that was a good sign. If he was dead, they'd cover him, wouldn't they?

Chapter Eight

The Cottage

Marci opened the oven door and checked the lasagna.

"It needs ten more minutes," said Jennifer, glancing at her watch.

"It looks done."

"Well, it isn't."

Marci took a fork and thrust it into the center, putting it into her mouth to test the heat. "Needs another ten minutes," she said, ignoring Jennifer's smug smile.

The table looked festive. Jennifer had obviously unpacked some of the old Christmas decorations, including a huge table centrepiece with bells and a miniature nativity scene. Marci wasn't one to celebrate Christmas once it was over. She couldn't understand the three month long holidays some people seemed to grant it. Oh well. She would be glad when this whole thing was over. She was happy to see her old college friends, but she would have preferred meeting them one on one, not in another one of Jennifer's contrived reunions. Her thoughts turned to Dena and her features softened as she pictured her the way she'd left her. A quick glance at Jennifer and she thrust Dena out of her thoughts. Somehow, she felt Jennifer could read her mind and she didn't want Jennifer to be a part of it, to sully the picture.

Karen had picked up their college yearbook from the end table and was thumbing through it, Sally sitting beside her and peering over her shoulder.

Sally suddenly laughed and pointed at a page. "The class prophecy," she said. "Can you even remember what they said about us all? I haven't thought about that in years."

"You were on the committee that wrote the prophecy, weren't you, Jennifer?"

"Along with Todd and Becky and Nash. It was Nash that did the writing. The rest of us only gathered the gossip for him."

"I'll bet," said Marci. She remembered when she'd first read the prophecy how she could almost hear Jennifer's voice reciting it.

Sally laughed again. "Listen to this. 'Our she-jock Karen will make history as the first athlete to win seven medals in both the winter and summer Olympics. She will retire on her sponsorships to a villa in Spain where she will breed Chihuahuas and train women, including her seven daughters, in track and field.'"

Marci noted Karen's laugh had a hollow ring and she wondered how much of a front she put on with her happy family pose. She remembered a different Karen, one willing to face challenges and explore new vistas. She looked around the room and thought they'd all got a little lost along the way. She felt suddenly content with her own life. She'd jumped her hurdles and was exactly where she wanted to be.

"Oh and look at this one," said Sally, caught up in the prophecy. "'Our bright and talented Marci, always at the head of the class no matter how untimely the assignments, will be basking in the glory of her second Nobel prize in science.'"

Marci forced a smile and tipped her glass in mock salute to Sally. "The Nobels are still in the future, I guess."

Karen chimed in. "Don't forget your own, Sally. 'Our Sally will become Earth Mother to her brood of children, writing her Pulitzer winning books along the way on the joys of parenting.' Oh, Sally, I'm sorry." Karen flung the book closed.

"It's all right, Karen. I've long since come to terms with the fact that Mac and I will never have children. I have a good life and God had other plans for me. As a pastor's wife, you must realize we take the life God gives us."

Sally picked up the book again and re-opened to the prophecy page. "Sophie. You're next. 'Our Sophie will become a race car driver and show all the male drivers what she's made of, winning both the Indy and the Grand Prix. In her spare time, she will tend her vineyard and develop a new line of super wines.'"

Sophie shot a dark look in Jennifer's direction and replied, "Sorry to disappoint on the super wines, but I could try for a new line of alcohol-free. One that doesn't taste like crap."

"On to Jennifer," said Sally, but she got no further as Jennifer announced loudly, "Time's up and the lasagna is ready." She pulled it out of the oven with bright red and green mitts and plunked it on the counter. "Salad is on the table, so if everyone takes a plate, we can dish our own and take a seat."

The yearbook fell to the floor as Sally and Karen joined the others in the kitchen. Will had been listening silently to the conversation, nearly invisible in his corner, but now he came out, first in line for the lasagna.

Chapter Nine

Marci
25 years earlier

Marci groaned and rolled over in her bed. "Turn out the light, I want to go back to sleep."

"You'll be late."

"Do I look like I care?" Four faces surrounded her bed and showed no intention of leaving her alone.

Marci wanted to block out the day. In fact, she wanted to block out the last three days. If only she could go back to Saturday, to a day when her life was going along in a perfect fashion. She and Becca had gone to a wedding. Becca's brother was the groom. It was the first time Marci had met their family and she thought things were going well. Then Becca had taken her aside after the ceremony when everyone was changing for the reception.

"Brian's friend Nick has asked me to marry him," she said.

Marci looked at her in astonishment. "What did you say? Why would he even ask you? Doesn't he know about us?"

"No one knows about us, Marci. I never told my family how things were between us."

Marci sat still and upright then, with a premonition of what was to come. She felt a shudder run down her spine. "What did you tell him?" she asked again.

"I told him I'd think about it."

"Why? How could you even think about it? I love you, Becca, and I thought you loved me too."

"I'm sorry, Marci. I just can't go on with our relationship. It would kill my dad if he knew about us."

"But what about you? What about me? Aren't we the ones that count?"

"Please don't make it difficult, Marci. Let's just end things and agree to be friends."

"Friends?" Marci's voice croaked. "We're not living in the fifties. Your parents will understand. Someday we might even be able to get married." Her voice trailed off as she realized Becca was no longer listening. Instead, her gaze was centered on the mirror above her dresser, at the school and family pictures that surrounded it. Marci followed her look and realized there wasn't a single picture there that included her.

"Were you ever going to tell them about us, Becca, or was I just a fling you took to get it out of your system before caving in to your family's plans for you?"

The coldness in Marci's voice must have made an impression. Becca's eyes misted, but she said firmly, "I'm sorry it turned out like this, Marci, but I want an ordinary life, a life with the picket fence and family dinners and—"

"You could have that with me. Do you really think you can live a lie for the rest of your life? What if Nick finds out about us? Can he live with a wife who doesn't love him?"

"I do love him in a way," said Becca. "We used to date in high school. We—"

Marci cut her off. "Justify it to yourself all you like, Becca, but you're making a big mistake and you'll ruin your life trying to be someone you aren't."

Becca stood then and Marci knew the conversation was over.

"I think I'll pass on the reception," she said. "Please give my regrets to your family. Say I came down sick suddenly. Say whatever you damn well please. I'm out of here."

Marci couldn't remember the drive back to the college. She knew she'd stopped at a bar on the way home and probably should have been stopped for drunk driving.

She remembered the trek down the hallway past the other rooms trying to make it home unseen. The door to Sally's room was open and all four were in there. She slithered past the entrance, made it to her own room at the end of the hall, closing her door firmly and throwing herself down on her bed, fully clothed. She didn't want to see anyone tonight.

The next thing she remembered was the sun shining and

she could smell coffee. The smell of eggs followed and she threw herself out of the bed and into the bathroom, curling herself around the porcelain as she upchucked all she'd eaten and drank the night before.

When she finished, she threw water on her face before she came face to face with Sally's smiling concern.

"You didn't show for breakfast and lunch is nearly over now, so I thought you could do with something to eat. But maybe not. How about some coffee?"

Marci shook her head and said, "Thanks but I couldn't really touch anything now. I just need to be alone." She fell face-down onto the bed again and heard Sally's footsteps retreating before she sat up. Sally had left the food, which she ignored, but she gulped the coffee and willed it to stay down.

She stayed there for the rest of the day.

Next morning was a repeat. This time, Marci was at least under the covers and in her pajamas. Sally left the food again after spending five minutes trying to engage an unresponsive Marci in conversation.

The third morning, all four of them piled into her room.

"So what is this, an intervention?" said Marci with a ghost of a smile.

"Something like that. You haven't eaten for three days."

"Two, actually."

"Whatever is wrong Marci, we're your friends and we want to help."

"I appreciate it, but no one can help. Just leave me alone."

"That's not how an intervention works, Marci. Now, first you hit the shower and get dressed. Then you're having at least coffee and toast and coming with us."

When she came out of the bathroom, the numbers had dwindled to Jennifer, Sophie, and Sally.

"Karen has a track meet today. Remember? We're all supposed to be giving her support, so we're bringing you along too."

Marci suddenly stopped still in the middle of the room. She felt the blood drain from her face.

"Today is Wednesday. I have a big paper due today. Karen's track meet was the same day. I forgot all about it.

It's major. If I don't turn in a paper, I'll fail the course."

"How close are you to being done?"

"Not close enough. I was going to finish it when I got back from Becca's." Her voice trailed off.

Sally opened her mouth to speak, but Jennifer interceded. "You and Sophie go along and I'll bring Marci in a few minutes. We'll meet you there."

While Marci sank down to her bed as the enormity of her omission hit her, Jennifer paced over to the window and stood looking out. The room was silent for a moment. Marci's thoughts for the first time in three days were on something other than her failed relationship. This could change the course of her career. She only had a couple of hours. She could never finish her partly completed paper in that time. With a fail, she'd have to take her course all over and it would follow her career for the rest of her life. How could she have been so stupid? How could she have forgotten?

When Jennifer turned back from the window, she said, "I might have an answer for you, Marci. I know someone who knows someone that might be able to help. If you want to try, it will stay between the two of us."

Marci shrugged. What did she have to lose?

Chapter Ten

The Cottage

They were all hungry, so conversation stagnated until the plates were nearly empty. Then Sophie broached the question they were all dying to ask.

"Okay, Jennifer, give. This isn't one of our regular reunions. You wanted us all here for a reason. What is it? Are you Woman of the Year again? Are you running for Parliament? Are you getting married?"

Jennifer slowly chewed a mouthful of salad and swallowed, wiping her mouth deliberately with a serviette before speaking.

"Don't be silly," she said, but Sophie noticed her hand gave an involuntary jerk as it slipped under the table. What was she hiding there? "It's been ages since we got together and I thought it was time. The week after Christmas is sort of depressing and anti-climatic, so what better idea than to hold this reunion on one of our old stomping grounds?" She paused and took a dramatic look around the cottage. "We did have some great times here. Remember the year we came here in the spring? The ice was barely off the lake and we decided to do a polar bear swim?"

Sophie noticed that even the silent Will smiled at that memory. He'd turned up that night to chop some firewood, and when he spotted the five of them clambering up the beach to the cottage in various states of undress, giggling and howling, he'd stood still as a lamppost with his jaw hanging. Sophie watched the flush creep up his face and remembered he hadn't been too quick to turn his eyes away. Of course, they had made quite a sight.

Marci laughed. "I remember fighting for the closest spots to the fireplace to warm up."

"It took hours for my teeth to stop chattering. And my bathing suit—I think it was stiff from being frozen," said Sally.

"I was so cold my bones hurt," added Karen. "Well, it's too early, or late, in the year to do a repeat. The ice will be thick on the lake. I think we'd die of hypothermia before we got to the shore anyhow. Let's think of some warmer visits."

Sophie looked around the table and wondered if she was the only one to realize how neatly Jennifer had turned the conversation from her question. Oh well, Jennifer would tell them all in her own good time. Sophie didn't really care about the answer. She only hated the way Jennifer used everything as a power play. She gave a rueful smile and glanced down at her glass of flavored sparkling water. She was surprised she'd even remembered the polar bear swim, considering the amount of alcohol she had probably consumed. Yet it stood out in vivid detail, right down to a picture of the clothes hanging to dry. She could remember what they had all been wearing and how they had arranged themselves in front of the fire. Maybe because that was the first time they'd partied together since the night at the gravel pit. Her nerves and senses were so raw, the time stood out from all the haze that went before and after.

Jennifer stood and began to stack the dirty plates. Sally jumped up to help and soon they were all clearing. Sophie started a pot of coffee and Jennifer pulled a plate from the fridge. "We're not done yet," she said. "Dessert is compulsory. No dieting, no refusals."

"Oooh, cherry cheesecake," breathed Marci. "Who would possibly refuse that?" She lifted a slice onto her plate and made orgasmic yelps of pleasure as she tasted the first bite.

"Remember the time we snuck a cherry cheesecake into the stacks at the library?" she asked. "We were having a great picnic. Then someone—you, I think, Sally—dropped cherries onto one of the reference books and we had a terrible time trying to clean it up. I'm sure it still has red stains on it somewhere in the depths of the reference section."

"I'm sure they figured out who the culprits were. We left dirty paper plates in the garbage can and everyone knew that was our regular spot. I'm surprised we didn't get a bill for book replacement or restoration. The no food or drink signs were posted everywhere."

Will had crossed to the door to look outside and opened it a crack. A blast of cold wind bearing hard pellets of snow whirled into the cottage. "Close the door, idiot!" they yelled in unison, then fell into a fit of giggles at Will's injured look. He compliantly closed the door after a brief glance outside.

"I was only checking to see if the storm was letting up."

"Well, obviously it isn't, so let's make the best of it," Jennifer said. "Coffee is ready. Who wants some?"

Sophie gave a sad glance at her pack of cigarettes and wondered if she was brave enough to venture into the cold for a smoke. Maybe she'd wait till the others were occupied and sneak one in the bathroom. She looked at Karen, who didn't seem to be suffering withdrawal, or maybe she was better at hiding it. Karen had never been one to show her feelings.

She glanced at the group, seated around the fireplace, all looking rather content in their reminiscences, and wondered why people always seemed to remember the good and minimize the bad.

Chapter Eleven

Sally
25 years ago.

Jennifer parked the car in the parking lot of the clinic and turned off the ignition. She put the keys in her purse and looked across to where Sally sat in the passenger seat, staring straight ahead, unmoving, unspeaking. Then Sally finally said, "I can't go through with it, Jennifer. It's all wrong."

Jennifer pulled in a long breath. "It's your decision. I'm only along for support. If you don't want to go through with it, we'll turn around now, go home, and cancel your appointment."

Still Sally remained seated. Jennifer drummed her fingers lightly on the steering wheel and waited too.

Finally, Sally made a quick motion to open the car door and jumped out. Jennifer smiled and followed.

Sally twitched and wriggled as she sat in the waiting room, feeling like a child in the principal's office waiting for a judgment. Only this judgment was a little more serious. What was she thinking?

Sally had always been the good girl. Her parents had drummed their morality into her and, even though she questioned it sometimes, it stayed with her. She had been the only virgin amongst the five friends. Sometimes she thought she was the only nineteen-year-old virgin left in the country.

What had possessed her to decide one night to rectify the situation? A few beers, probably. She wasn't much of a drinker and the alcohol had affected her more than she anticipated. It was definitely true that it lowered your inhibitions. So when the very eligible football jock Carl began to pay her more attention than usual at a party one night, dancing and flirting with her, then pulling her off down the hall to a bedroom, she had given a mental shrug. What the heck. She had to lose her virginity sometime. It might as well be with Carl.

How stupid could I be? she wondered. Everyone else was on the pill, but not virginal Sally. She couldn't even blame Carl for not having protection. He probably assumed she was on the pill, like every other intelligent female primate.

The lovemaking, if that's what you would call a secretive, drunken fumble in a strange bedroom, was anything but satisfactory. Through the sudden searing pain as her hymen broke, Sally began to sob. Carl had climaxed and his grin of satisfaction changed quickly to a "What the F? You never said you were a virgin." He scrambled with his clothes to the bathroom, leaving Sally to cope with the mess. Too late she realized a towel strategically placed would have helped matters. She gave a sigh of relief to see the coat they were lying on was her own.

She had sobered instantly. Rolling her coat into a ball to hide the evidence, she checked to be sure no signs of her lost virginity were visible on the bedspread or other coats. She peered around the corner. No one was paying attention. Carl had left the bathroom. She could hear his voice, loud and laughing, in the living room. She managed to make herself presentable in the bathroom, but couldn't face the party. Maybe Carl had told them all about her. Maybe that's what he was laughing about. But another part of her knew he had already put her out of his mind. Tomorrow he probably wouldn't even remember.

Jennifer had spotted her coming out of the bathroom and she had blurted out the whole sorry story, sitting on the floor outside the bathroom door. Jennifer pulled on her own coat and found a sweater for Sally. She coaxed Sally back to the party room. They skirted the group and Jennifer shouted over the din to the cries of "party-pooper."

"Sally's a bit under the weather, we're going home." Carl never even looked in their direction.

Sally stayed in bed the next day, claiming the flu or a hangover, depending on who inquired. She never told anyone else and didn't even ask Jennifer if she had passed on the story to the others. From their actions over the next weeks, she gathered that Jennifer had kept her secret, even from their friends.

Sally had thought it was all over and done with until the day she realized her period was late. For a week she watched and waited. The only person she could confide in was Jennifer, who already knew the sordid details. Jennifer advised her to wait a little longer. Maybe the stress had delayed her period. That happened sometimes. But Sally knew. By the time she was certain, Jennifer had found her the right doctor to see and went along for support for the original appointment.

Now here she was, taking care of things. But taking care of things meant ridding herself of her baby. Other girls did it. The ones, like her, too stupid to use birth control. But Sally was so conflicted she changed her mind nearly every day. Her emotions were a mess of guilt, frustration, and a why-me anger. Jennifer said, "It's your hormones. They're making you emotional. Just ride them through. It will soon be over."

The nurse in a starchy blue uniform looked in her direction. "Sally, the doctor is ready for you now."

Jennifer squeezed her hand. "It will soon be over," she repeated. "I'll wait for you."

Sally stood obediently, chasing all her guilt aside with rationalizations. She could never give a baby the things it needed. She could never face her family. She could never face her friends or finish college. She gave an involuntary sob and the nurse looked at her quickly, but she pasted a smile on her face and went on.

It was over quickly. But it would never be really over. Sally developed an infection. How could she get an infection in that sterile environment? But she did, and the result was that the aborted pregnancy was the only one she would ever have.

It was nearly a week before Sally could sleep through the night without waking to find tears streaming down her face. Jennifer suggested a psychologist or student counsellor, but Sally knew no amount of counselling would chase away the guilt. She'd have to learn to live with it on her own.

Chapter Twelve

The Cottage

Sophie drained her coffee cup and took a longing look at the bathroom. She intercepted a glance from Jennifer that said she knew exactly what she was thinking and shrugged.

"I'm going out for a smoke," she said. "Anyone want to come?" Karen, the only other smoker, shook her head. Sophie took her parka from the hook by the door, pulled up her fur-lined hood, and zipped about three zippers against the cold. She pulled a cigarette from the pack, along with her lighter, and pulled on her boots.

"You're wearing those?" asked Karen, taking in the tall slender heels, made for fashion, not for winter hiking.

"All I've got," answered Sophie nonchalantly.

"I never knew you were such a fashion maven," piped in Marci.

"It's my one weakness when it comes to clothes. I have a shoe fetish."

"I remember," said Sally. "Your closet was always full of shoes. You used to wear the most outrageous shoes and then top them off with jeans and a t-shirt."

"Everyone has to have at least one idiosyncrasy." Sophie opened the door to another burst of snow and cold, shutting it quickly behind her before she got a chorus of protests.

"Sophie's managed to stay on the wagon for quite a while this time," said Karen when the door had closed. "I hope she's finally shaken off her demons."

"We all have demons to shake," said Sally with uncharacteristic gloom. "Do they ever totally go away?"

"Well, I'm for another glass of wine," said Marci. "Any

other imbibers ready for more?"

Everyone except Will held up an empty glass for a refill. He gave Marci a negative salute with his half full glass. "I'll have to open a new one," said Marci. "There's some red left here, but we need a new white."

"Let's sort out the sleeping arrangements," said Jennifer. "Then we can get rid of that pile of luggage." She motioned to the pile of assorted bags they had all dumped by the far wall of the living area. "Sally, you and Karen can take the far room. Marci and Sophie can have the room with the moose head and I'll take the little one with the single bed. Will, sorry, but you have to settle for the couch."

While Marci opened and poured the wine, the others moved their cases into their assigned rooms. No one thought to complain that Jennifer automatically assumed the single room. After all, it was her cottage. Will helped them move.

"I don't even have a toothbrush," he grumbled.

"Well, you're not borrowing mine," said Jennifer. "I have some mouthwash unopened. You can pour out some for yourself, but that's as far as I go." She disappeared into her room to get the bottle and handed it to him.

"I'm going down to check the water pipe where it comes in to the cottage. It had a bit of a leak earlier, but I think I got it bunged up." No one was listening to his statement, so Will set the bottle of mouthwash on the counter, grabbed his jacket, and headed for the cellar.

Karen went to the bathroom, and the others began to unpack their clothes. In Sophie's absence, Marci chose the bed closest to the door. There was a good draft coming in through the window and Marci liked a warm, cozy bed. She also took the two top drawers of the dresser. Sophie, except for her shoes, always traveled light when it came to wardrobe, so one drawer and the remaining hangers would be enough for her.

Sally unpacked on her own. She took one more try at her cell phone to see if she could get reception. She'd really like to hear Mac's voice even for a moment. Now was her chance to be alone, with Karen taking her extended smoke break in the bathroom. She giggled and wondered if Jennifer would be sniffing as she passed the bathroom door. She flung her phone down in disgust. She wouldn't get a line out until they left here and made it out as far as the highway. She could try the land line, but didn't want to talk to Mac with everyone listening.

After they had all unpacked and returned to the living room, Will took the remaining case, assuming it must be Sophie's, into the moose-head room. "Sophie must be smoking half the pack to make up for lost time," he said. "Doesn't she feel the cold? She's going to be frostbitten if she doesn't come in."

"Go yell at her out the door. She must be done with her cigarette by now." All five of them stopped as though with a common thought. Jennifer repeated, more seriously now, "Will, go get Sophie." The others exchanged worried looks.

"She's been gone a long time," said Karen. "Do you think she could have wandered off looking for something, maybe out to her car? It's down the drive a ways. She might get lost in the snow."

Will was only out for a minute when he gave a sudden shout, muffled against the wind but still audible. Jennifer ran to the door, followed by the others. Will pushed the door open part way. "She fell," he said. "She must have hit her head on something. She's hurt pretty bad. Help me bring her in. Or at least hold the door. I can lift her myself."

They stood in the cold, waiting for Will. He came in, dangling Sophie over his shoulder in a fireman's lift and, kneeling beside the couch, he laid her out. They crowded around. "Sophie, Sophie!" Jennifer was closest to her head and slapped her face lightly, trying to get her to move. They could all see the large gash on her head and the blood seeping from it.

"She's not moving. I don't think she's breathing." Jennifer put her face close to Sophie's and then held her finger at Sophie's neck. "There's no pulse," she said, leaning back on her heels and looking at the others, horror-struck. "I think she's dead."

Karen took one of Sophie's limp wrists and felt for a sign of life, but shook her head. Marci fumbled in her purse and produced a mirror. She held it in front of Sophie's mouth. No mist formed on the glass.

They all sat back, looking at each other, stunned and uncomprehending.

"Where was she, Will?"

"She was at the side where I was chopping firewood earlier. I think she must have fallen. There's a slippery spot there that's almost solid ice from where water dripped off the roof last week in that warm spell. The snow has just blown over it. She must have slipped on that and fallen against the axe. It was stuck in the chopping block."

"It doesn't look like she fell on something as sharp as an axe," said Jennifer.

"It wasn't sharp," said Will. "It was the blunt end she would have fallen against."

"Would that really be enough to kill her?"

"If she fell hard enough, I guess. It must have. What other explanation can there be?"

No one could think of any other explanation. They exchanged looks of helplessness that traveled around the room.

"We can't leave her here," said Jennifer. "Will, take her and lay her out in the bedroom." Will obliged. The others sat silently, trying to comprehend the incomprehensible. A few minutes ago, Sophie had been laughing with them, and now she was dead.

Karen picked up the wine bottle and topped everyone off. "Is there any sense trying the phone again?" she asked.

Sally picked hers up. "No signal. There's nothing we can do for Sophie until we can get out of here."

Marci jerked her head up suddenly. "Where did you put Sophie, Will?"

He shrugged. "On the bed where her luggage was."

"I can't spend the night with her," said Marci in a trembling voice. "I'll have to move my things into one of the other rooms."

"My bed's only a single," said Jennifer.

"There's space in our room," said Karen. "The beds are both twins, but we can make one up with blankets on the floor. Or we could scrunch up in one of the twins." She said the last with a reluctant air that Marci knew was only a token offer.

"I'll pack my things up and bring them along," agreed Marci, not following her words with action.

"Oh," said Karen suddenly. "I have sleeping bags in the

car. I always travel with them in the winter, in case I get
stuck in the cold. They'll be a lot more comfortable than
blankets on the floor. I'll go get them."

"I'm all right with blankets," said Marci. "It's too cold to
go out to the car and dangerous in the snow."

"My car is just on the other side of Sally's. I can see the
lights the way there and back. It will only take a minute.
Then we'll warm the sleeping bags by the fire for a bit."

Marci finally agreed. She didn't really want to share a bed
with Karen. She'd rather sleep on the floor. She made a
move to go after her things in the bedroom. She packed
quickly, not turning on the overhead light. She couldn't bear
to look at Sophie's still form on the other bed.

Karen pulled on her boots and parka. Will followed her
outside. "I need to top up the firewood," he said. The door
opened with a fierce bang and they ran outside quickly, pulling it shut behind them.

Chapter Thirteen

Karen
25 years earlier

Karen threw her bank passbook into her desk drawer in disgust. She'd never have enough in savings to make it through her last year. Her student loans were already maxed. What she wanted—no, needed—was that athletic scholarship.

She already spent most of her free hours on the track, training. Her coach told her she was overtraining. She should take time off to relax and let her body adjust between sessions. Her friends told her the same thing. She ignored the advice.

If it weren't for Tammy Wade, she knew she would have the scholarship locked up. Karen's dorm mirror was covered in beribboned medals she had won throughout her sports career, going back to grade school. But Tammy had the same, with a few records thrown in, better than hers. And there was only one track scholarship for women at this college.

The last big meet of the year tomorrow would decide who got the scholarship and Karen had to have it, even if she fell at the finish line, lapsing into a coma as a result. Her lips twitched in a bitter semi-smile at the picture. Tammy didn't need it the way she did. Tammy's family was rolling in money—they owned half the real estate in the small college town. Karen didn't have the luxury of family money; she didn't even have the luxury of family. She had to make her way on her own, and the scholarship was her ticket to a future.

She looked up to see Jennifer standing in her open doorway, watching her with an expression of concern. "Karen, you're strung tighter than a pro tennis racquet. Come out with us. We're going to Dennis's house for a party."

"I'll pass, thanks. I need to get some sleep. I have to get up early to—"

"No you don't." Jennifer walked across the room and took Karen gently by the arm. "You know you're overdoing it, and it's not going to help. It's counterproductive. Take a night to relax. You don't have to drink. You don't even have to stay late. Just come and listen to some music and dance and socialize. It will help you sleep and help you tomorrow."

And Karen had let herself be shepherded along. She didn't feel as though she had the strength to resist Jennifer's logic. And in her heart of hearts, she knew it was true. She wouldn't be at her best tomorrow if she couldn't get her body out of its current state of unrest.

The beer was flowing, the music a little loud, and the conversation came from all directions when they arrived, Jennifer having stopped to round up the rest of their group. The first person Karen noticed was Tammy. Tammy's eyes swung up to meet hers and they exchanged smiles. Tammy lifted a glass in salute. Karen couldn't make out if it was beer or a soft drink. She was pretty sure Tammy was as serious about the meet as she was, so she would bet on ginger ale.

An hour later, Karen was ready to go home. She took a bathroom run, determined to leave, not letting the others convince her to stay. The bathroom door was locked, so she waited in the corridor just outside. A few seconds later, Jennifer popped out.

"All yours," she said.

"I'm going to head home now," said Karen. "The rest of you stay; I'll call a cab."

Jennifer ignored her statement, pulling her into the bathroom instead. "Here's something that would solve all your problems," she said, opening the bathroom cabinet with a giggle. She pointed to a pack of laxatives, super strength. "A dose or two of that in Tammy's drink would do the trick for the morning." Then she giggled again. "Oh," she said, as she started to leave. "Don't call a cab. If you give us a half hour or so, we'll all be ready to go too. The party isn't as good as I thought. Apparently, the neighbors made a noise complaint, so the cops have been driving by. Not a good start to a party."

Karen stood still for a moment, staring at the package Jennifer had pointed out. She snorted in disgust at herself. How could she even consider doing something so under-handed? She needed the scholarship, but she needed to get it honestly. She slammed the cabinet door shut and sat down for a pee. But as she washed her hands, all she could think about was the innocent enough package on the cabinet shelf. Someone knocked on the bathroom door. "Are you done in there yet?" asked a male voice. Karen quickly made her deci-sion and bolted from the bathroom.

The next day, when Tammy was announced as a non-starter due to illness, Jennifer was the only one who locked eyes on Karen. No accusations, just a steady, understanding look.

The scholarship got Karen through her last year, much good that it did her. Two months after graduation, she mar-ried Terry and left her job to become an old-fashioned wife and mother, raising the two girls and leaving the rest to Ter-ry. She tried to put the memory of that night out of her mind, but every time they had one of their reunions, she could picture Jennifer's unspoken words of conspiracy.

Chapter Fourteen

The Cottage

"I'm going to move some of my things so Marci can have more room in the drawers," said Sally. She realized she was talking to empty air. Jennifer had retreated to the bathroom and Sally could hear her gargling loudly.

She cleared a drawer and pushed some things to the side in the closet. None of them had packed heavily, so there was lots of room. A few minutes later, Marci came in, shutting the door quickly behind her. Her face was white.

"Are you all right?" asked Sally, reaching to touch her arm. "You're freezing. Let's go out to the fire. You can unpack later."

"I'm all right," said Marci. "It's just the terrible thoughts going through my head."

"We all feel terrible about Sophie, of course."

"It's not just that. It's how I felt, being around her. I couldn't stand to be in the room with her. It's as though she stopped being a person and suddenly became a thing." She sat down on the end of the bed and sobbed into her hands. Sally sat beside her, her arm around the shaking shoulders, crooning to her as though she were a child.

A tap came to the door. "Are you all right?" Jennifer's voice was low and concerned.

"Fine," answered Sally. "We're coming out now." She tugged at Marci's arm and she stood with her, pulling her hand across her damp eyes. Sally handed her a tissue. Repairs made, they went out to the living room.

Will came through the door with an armful of firewood. "Can someone help me with the door?" he shouted over the howling wind. Jennifer and Sally both rushed over. Jennifer got there first and held it while Will rescued his tumbling armful of wood. She shut it as quickly as she could.

"Hasn't Karen come back yet?" she asked.

"Not that I've seen. We were in the bedroom. I didn't hear her come in."

"Will, didn't you see her? You were outside."

"I was around the corner, getting the wood." He still had his coat and boots on, so he slid outside the door. They could hear him yelling, "Karen!"

Jennifer took the remaining coats in her arm and took them to the seat beside the fireplace. "Nothing is going to dry out by the door," she said. "Look, all the coats are still covered in snow."

"So are the boots," said Sally, picking up two pairs and bringing them to the fireside as well.

They looked up as the door opened, expecting Karen and Will, but only Will stood there, a frozen look on his face.

"What the hell is going on?" he asked finally. "Who's been out of the cottage?"

"No one," they said together.

"Well, someone has. Unless you believe there's a Yeti out there with a grudge against us."

"Sit down, Will," said Jennifer in her most commanding voice. "What's wrong and what have you done with Karen?"

"I haven't done anything with Karen," he said. "But someone has."

Silence hung like an invisible cloak.

"She's been killed," he said finally.

The three women ran as one to the doorway, surrounding Will, waiting for explanation.

"She's out there. By her car. On the ground, and she's dead."

"Maybe she fell," began Sally with faltering hope in her voice. "Maybe she's just hurt and can't get up. We have to go bring her in."

She began to push her way past Will, then looked wonderingly at the empty coat hooks before making a move to the couch where they lay drying.

Will put out an arm to restrain her. "She didn't fall. Or at least that's not what killed her." He stopped, took a big gulp of air, and went on. "She has a knife stuck into her side and there's blood all around her. She's dead. There's no doubt."

"We have to bring her in," said Jennifer. "We can't just leave her out there."

"It's a crime scene," said Will. "The police won't want us to touch anything."

"I don't care a fig what the police want. Karen is out there. She's our friend and we're not going to leave her lying there. It could be days before we can get the police."

A look of horror swept Sally's face. "Days?" she asked weakly. "Surely someone will come tomorrow. We can't stay here for days. Not with Sophie and Karen...." She couldn't go on.

Jennifer laid a comforting arm around her shoulder. "You and Marci stay here together. Sit on the couch and get warm. Will and I are going to bring Karen in. Crime scene or no crime scene, she's coming inside."

She grabbed her coat, quickly pulled on her boots, and exited with Will into the howling wind.

Sally and Marci huddled together on the couch. "You know what this means," said Marci.

"What?" Sally lifted a tear-stained face.

"There's no one here but the four of us. Roads are closed. No one can get in. Even if someone had a snowmobile, how could they even find us in the blowing snow? Sally, one of us has to be a killer."

They sat in stunned silence for a minute.

"But why?" asked Sally. "Why would anyone want to kill Karen?"

"Not just Karen, but Sophie too."

"She fell."

"Did she now? It seems a little strange to imagine her falling in such an exact way that she hit her head on the blunt end of the axe."

"You're right." Sally shivered in spite of the heat coming from the burning logs. "We made ourselves believe that she fell, but now, with Karen dead, it can't be a coincidence. Someone must have done it."

"One of us," affirmed Marci.

They waited for the door to open. It seemed ages before it swung open with a wild bang against the wall. Sally and Marci both jumped up. Will and Jennifer had arranged a sort of sled with the sleeping bag Karen had gone out for. They dragged her in along with a mound of snow, leaving her on the floor as they closed the door and pulled off their boots.

Sally stifled a nearly hysterical giggle at the sight. *Our training stays with us,* she thought. *No matter we are dragging our murdered friend, we still have to stop and wipe our feet.* She suppressed her giggle immediately at the sight of the blood covering Karen and now the sleeping bag.

Jennifer said, "Will and I will put her in the bedroom with Sophie. Sally, Marci, make some coffee. We have to sit down and talk."

Marci put on the coffee. Sally rinsed out their dinner cups and wiped them. Jennifer and Will came out of the hallway to the bedrooms as the coffee was still coming down. The carafe was nearly full, so Marci ignored the drip still oozing out and poured four cups, replacing the container on the element to finish its download.

The four all took a gulp or two of coffee before anyone spoke. Will rubbed his hands and held them in front of the fire. Jennifer clutched the hot cup as though warming hers.

Sally was the first to speak. "Is there no way Karen could have had a terrible accident? Like Sophie?" She couldn't bear the thought of the conversation that was to come.

Jennifer gave her a scornful look. "Neither of them had a terrible accident. They were killed—murdered, both of them."

"But who?" Sally had never liked drawn out conflicts. She liked to get the terrible things over with quickly. But she knew this one wasn't going to go away in a hurry.

Marci was the one who answered this time. "It has to be one of us." Sally noticed they all reacted the same. No direct eye contact. Instead, each of them surreptitiously let their glances slide from one to the other of their group. Marci went on. "No one can get in or out, right?"

A silent chorus of nods.

"So, we just have to figure out which one of us is a murderer." She laughed, a short staccato sound that inhaled coffee and subsided in a coughing fit.

When she recovered, Jennifer said, "She's right. But how? We've been together nearly all the time. How could anyone slip away without being seen?"

Marci had recovered now enough to speak. "We have to

remember what each of us was doing when Sophie went out for her cigarette, and what each of us was doing when Karen went out. One of us must have some time unaccounted for, and that one is the killer. I'll start," she said. "When Sophie went out, I was putting my things away in the bedroom. Since Sophie was outside, I was alone. I could hear Karen in the bathroom."

"I don't think we need to worry about Karen's whereabouts," said Jennifer a little acidly. "After all, she didn't knife herself, so I don't think she killed Sophie. It's bizarre enough to think one of us might be a killer without considering two of us."

Will waited for someone else to speak and, when no one did, he cleared his throat. "I was here in the living room for a bit. Then I went down to the cellar to look for some old blankets to pile around the front door. Something to stop the draft."

"I don't see any blankets," said Jennifer, pointedly staring at the door.

"I couldn't find any."

"There should be some in that old cupboard in the far end. Probably musty, but they'd do to block the draft."

"I tried that. It wouldn't open. It must be locked."

"It can't be," said Jennifer. "There's never been a lock on it."

"Well, stuck fast then."

The others watched this dialogue in varying stages of disbelief. Two friends were lying dead in the other room and they were arguing about a lock.

Finally, Sally brought them back to the question and said, "I unpacked, alone in the bedroom. Then I tried to call Mac in case the phone had service again. It didn't."

Jennifer was the last. "I dug out the mouthwash for Will and then I unpacked in my room alone, with the door shut. It looks as though that's what we all did. And with no one in the living room." She looked hard at Will. "No one could say if one of us slipped out of a bedroom or a bathroom, or the cellar, and went outside to cosh Sophie."

"What about Karen?" asked Will. "Where were we all then? I was outside chopping wood. My back was to the door. Anyone could have gone in or out and I wouldn't have seen or heard anything in the noise of the storm."

Sally said, "I went to the bedroom to move some things around so that Marci had room in the drawers and closet. She couldn't stay in the room alone with Sophie. Then when you came in, Marci, we were together for a while. You were so white and cold."

"I was upset," said Marci. "I didn't slip out and kill Karen! I was cold because I was in shock."

Jennifer said, "I was in the bathroom, brushing my teeth and washing up. I didn't hear anything except for the wind."

Everyone turned to Will again. Marci put thought to words for all of them. "You were outside when Karen was killed, the only one who was outside. You were supposedly in the cellar when Sophie died. No one else could have done it."

"Don't be ridiculous," said Will. "Why would I ever want to hurt either of them? I don't even know them. Jennifer is the only one of you I really know. And she's still alive and well."

Sally felt like clutching at straws. "Is there no way anyone could get in? Could someone have been waiting outside, just to pick us off one by one as we go out?"

"Why?" asked Marci. "Why would anyone want to kill us?"

"Why would one of us? My question isn't any more far-fetched than that." Sally slumped into her seat.

Beside her, Marci sat bolt upright. "The car!" she said. "The car that was in the ditch. Out by the road."

"What car?" asked Jennifer. "No one said anything about a car."

Marci explained. "There was a car in the ditch out by where the road turns. It was all covered in snow and no one was inside. It was probably abandoned when the storm started."

"It wasn't there when I came," said Jennifer thoughtfully.

"Or me," said Sally, then added doubtfully, "At least I don't think so. I was concentrating on the road. I might not have seen it."

"It wouldn't matter," said Will. "No one could wait in a stalled car all this time. They'd be frozen to death long ago."

"I stopped when I saw it," said Marci. "And I checked to be sure no one was inside. It was empty."

"Well there you go," said Will. "Someone got a ride be-

fore the road was totally impassible. He's probably sitting in
front of a nice warm fire now."

"What kind of a car was it?" asked Jennifer. Sally scanned
her face. She recognized Jennifer's expression of studied
casualness. Usually it meant she was about to drop a bomb-
shell.

"A dark blue Buick. It looked new. That's all I could see.
It was already starting to cover with snow."

Sally could have sworn Jennifer's hand twitched. "And
you're sure no one was in it?" she asked.

"Positive. I checked in the back seat as well. Oh, and
there was no key in the ignition."

They sat without speaking for a few minutes. Sally could
almost hear the gears turning in everyone's head. Jennifer
was the first to break the silence. "I don't like that car out by
the road. Let's be sure before we start accusing each other.
There's an outside entrance to the cellar. Is there any way
someone could have been hiding in there all along, just going
out when one of us did?"

They all jumped up, glad of another possibility. "All right.
Just the two of us will check. Marci, you and Sally stay here
and Will and I will check the cellar."

"But if it is one of us, we should all stay together," protested Sally.

Jennifer gave a bitter laugh. "Well if we stay in pairs and
one of us is killed, we'll know who the killer is, won't we?"

"It's nothing to joke about," said Marci.

Will and Jennifer took to the stairs. Will grabbed a flash-
light. "There's only one bulb down there and I think it's on its
last leg."

Marci took two glasses of wine from the kitchen counter
and handed one to Sally."I don't remember whose is whose,
but I don't think someone else's germs is at the top of our
list of worries right now."

They sat together, sipping slowly at the wine. Sally
looked sideways at Marci, but she was staring straight ahead.
"My bet is on Will," Marci said. "How could anyone else have
slipped out? He was the one with the best chance."

"But what reason would he have? He barely knows any of
us except for Jennifer," said Sally. "The rest of us know each
other very well. Maybe too well."

Now Marci turned to give her full attention to Sally. "What does that mean? Do you really think one of us would have a reason to kill two women who have been our best friends since college?"

Sally sighed. "No, I guess not. Now if Jennifer was the one killed, it would be more believable."

Marci gave a snort, but didn't disagree with her. "Jennifer liked her secrets. We all had them and, somehow, she always became part of the cover-up. I see what you mean." She digested the thought for a moment and went on. "But if any of us wanted to kill to keep a secret, wouldn't we have done it years ago? And Karen and Sophie weren't the secret blabbing types."

"You're right." The admission came from Sally a little grudgingly. "Sophie likely had some memory holes from our last year in college. She wasn't in good shape. I'm surprised she even made her courses. And Karen, she was always the most private one of us all."

The cellar door opened. Will and Jennifer had returned from their reconnaissance. They were each clutching a comforter. Jennifer said, "There's no one down there now. But there was a clump or two of snow by the outside entrance." She took the blanket from Will and set them close to the fire. "We did manage to get the cupboard open. The door was just stuck."

"I told you. That snow was from when I came in the outside cellar door to get the axe."

"It might not be. There might have been someone hiding out down there."

"Then where is he now? Out having a wienie roast by the lake?"

"Sarcasm doesn't go well on you, Will. I'm just trying to find a scenario that would explain things. Otherwise, what do we have? One of us is killing the others? That's preposterous."

"What do we do now?" interrupted Sally.

"We stay together," said Jennifer, in a voice that brooked no nonsense. "Gather blankets and pillows and we'll all bunk down in this room in front of the fire. If we stay together, no one can pick off stragglers."

"I don't know about that," said Sally. "Have you never

read Agatha Christie? One of her books, *And Then There Were None,* takes place on this deserted island and everyone gets killed one at a time, even though they are—"

"I don't think we need murder mysteries tonight," Jennifer interrupted firmly. "This storm can't last forever. It should start clearing tomorrow. We just take care not to be alone tonight and in the morning, we start trying again to make contact. Maybe the phone lines will be up again. Maybe a plough will come through."

Even the usually confident Jennifer wasn't able to insert much enthusiasm into her hopes.

They made forays into the bedrooms gathering pillows, comforters, and sheets. No one dallied for long and no one closed a door behind them while they collected belongings. Soon they had four beds arranged in a semicircle around the warmth of the fire. The extra blankets Jennifer and Will had brought up from the cellar were now warm and added to the mix.

"What about the bathroom?" asked Sally.

"What about the bathroom?" Jennifer threw back at her.

"If we have to go in the night, do we wake someone up or just go alone?"

"Since the bathroom is only a few feet away, I don't think a trip is going to put anyone in danger. But everyone go now and then hold it till morning."

"That means no more coffee or wine." Sally pushed her glass away. Then she got up to collect the other empty glasses and put them in the kitchen sink. "We can wash up in the morning, I guess."

"You think?" said Marci. "Who cares about the state of the cottage when we might not wake up in the morning?"

"There has to be an explanation," said Sally, clutching at straws. "Maybe Sophie was an accident, and maybe Karen..." But she couldn't go on. No possibility came to mind.

They began as one to huddle in their makeshift beds. Will jumped up to turn out the light.

"No," said Jennifer. "The light stays on. I don't care if the light bothers anyone, but I'm not falling asleep in the dark."

No one argued. Sally could hear everyone breathing, almost in unison. All four lying on their backs, staring at the ceiling.

Chapter Fifteen

Jennifer
25 years ago

The party was getting boring. Jennifer sat in one corner of the house surrounded by her usual entourage—Sally, Karen, Marci, and two football jocks that had been trying to put the moves on Sally and Marci respectively. Jennifer could tell they were both going to strike out. Sally was that modern day anomaly of a "good girl, saving herself for marriage," and Marci had other fish to fry. Still, it amused her to watch. Sophie had disappeared with her current boyfriend Michael. He drank nearly as much as she did, so they made a good pair. She'd keep an eye on them later. Neither would be in fit state to drive and Michael had brought his Camaro.

A newcomer joined their group at the outskirts. She looked a little lost and out of place. Jennifer recognized her— Laura Somers. She smiled at her and got a wide returning smile of gratitude.

"Not the liveliest party tonight," she said.

"I don't usually go to parties. I always feel out of place," said Laura. Jennifer examined her carefully as she talked. She was a pretty girl in a non-striking way—blonde hair, natural, little makeup, and expensive but old-fashioned clothes. She came from money, Jennifer knew.

Another thing she knew about Laura was that she was a brain. She didn't look it. She looked like a clingy helpless type that needed the opinion of a man to tell her what to wear. But looks could be deceiving.

"My brother Aaron is always at me to go out, so I told

him I was coming to a class party just to get him off my back." She sighed and took a small sip of her drink. She quickly took another, her discomfort at her surroundings quite apparent.

Jennifer talked to Laura with one eye scanning the crowd. Nelson Benson should be making an appearance. Jennifer had short-listed him on her manifest of possible boyfriends. The trouble was, she hadn't been able to get a rise out of him yet. She usually had no difficulty getting whoever she wanted to ask her out. The main difficulty had been getting rid of them when she was bored. Nelson was different, and the more he ignored her, the more intrigued with him she became.

She spotted him. He'd arrived alone. Good start. Now she had to get his attention without looking as though she wanted it. She joined the conversations around her, more enthusiastically than she had been, flirting with the two jocks who were beginning to realize they were striking out with their intended targets, throwing her head back in a burst of laughter.

From the corner of her eye, she could see Nelson tracking laterally through the room. She was pretty sure she knew his destination. He stopped in front of her group, holding up a beer can in a sort of salute. "Mind if I join you?" he asked.

Jennifer shrugged and moved aside to give him room to sit on the huge sofa. He sat on the floor instead, in front of Jennifer and Laura, facing them and leaning against a coffee table he shoved out of the way behind him, setting a black leather pouch on the floor beside him.

"What is that?" asked Laura, pointing at the pouch, black box sliding out to the floor.

He grinned and pulled it the rest of the way out. "It's an old Polaroid I found in our garage. Remember these?" He pointed it in Laura's direction and snapped. "Just wait a minute," he said. "This one belonged to my old man. He used to bring it to my little league games and take pictures of our team. I'd forgotten all about it until I saw it tonight looking for something else." He watched till the photo rolled out of the camera and snapped it off. "See? I thought it would be fun to bring to a party."

Sophie had straggled back to the group minus Michael and sat on the floor beside Nelson, tossing back her beer and looking around for a source to get another. Miraculously, one appeared in front of her outstretched hand. Michael had followed her.

"Oh, a Polaroid! I haven't seen one of those in ages," she said. "Come on, Nelson, take one of the Fab Five for us." Sophie bounced onto the couch between Jennifer and Sally, ignoring Laura on the other side of Jennifer.

Jennifer, Sophie, Marci, Karen, and Sally all crowded together. "You too," said Nelson to Laura as he readied to take the picture. He took one and they waited impatiently to see it. As it began to develop, he handed it to Laura. She smiled at it for a moment then passed it down the line. When they'd all had a look, Jennifer popped it into her purse. Attention spans at a party are short. No one noticed or cared what happened to the picture once they'd seen it.

She was getting a little annoyed with the pasty-faced Laura. Who would think she would appeal to Nelson? Well, if that's how he wanted it, she was about to lose interest in him. There were plenty more fish in the sea. Nelson slipped off to get a drink. Jennifer decided if the party didn't pick up shortly, she'd call it a night and head home. Karen was trying to get her attention, looking at her watch, and Sally never liked parties much anyhow. Marci, she knew, had a big paper due and had to have her arm twisted to come in the first place. The trick would be getting Sophie to come with them. Jennifer liked to see all her chicks home to roost.

Laura began to rummage in her purse, looking for something she didn't seem able to lay her hands on. "What are you looking for?" asked Jennifer a little crossly, smarting from the rebuff she'd received from Nelson.

"I have a headache," she said. "But I can't find my aspirin."

"I can't help you there."

"I can," piped up Michael. "Here." He slipped his hand into his pocket and pulled out a plastic pouch with little pills in it. "Take one of these. They'll cure what ails you."

"They don't look like aspirin," said Laura. "What are they?"

"Better than aspirin. They'll cure your headache fast."

Sophie broke into a giggle, then held out her hand and quickly swallowed the one Michael gave her. Jennifer opened her mouth to discourage Laura, but she reached for the pill and popped it down before the words came out.

Later, Jennifer wondered if she really tried hard enough to stop Laura from taking the pill. She could have just reached out and stopped her, couldn't she? Maybe it was her fault, what happened later. Maybe she was upset with Laura for stealing her thunder and didn't try hard enough. Maybe she thought if she was naive enough to take a pill at a party from a perfect stranger, she deserved the aftermath. She never realized what that aftermath would be.

Was that why she'd kept the Polaroid photo all these years, slipped into the back cover of an old album? On the back, she'd written the date with Laura's name, and the names of the five friends on there as well.

Chapter Sixteen

The Cottage

Jennifer came awake with a start. She hadn't intended to fall asleep in the first place. She could hear the others breathing, but not the long shallow breaths of sleep. "Is anyone awake?" she whispered quietly.

"Yes," whispered Sally. "I can't sleep at all."

"Me neither," said Marci. "I'm just lying here waiting for the axe to fall. So to speak," she added when she realized what she'd actually said.

Will grunted, but it didn't sound like a sleepy grunt.

"We might as well sit up if no one is going to sleep," said Jennifer.

"We should check outside and see if the wind and snow are letting up," said Marci.

"No way is that door opening until daylight," said Jennifer. "Who knows what's on the other side."

"No one could be waiting out there in the cold," said Will.

"I know that logically," said Jennifer. "But I'm still more comfortable with it shut."

"It doesn't sound as wild as it was," said Sally. "Maybe in a few hours it will be over and a plough or something will come by."

Will said, "I wouldn't hold your breath. They'll do the highway and the more populated areas first, so school buses can get through."

"There's no school!" said Sally. "We're in the middle of Christmas holidays."

"Oh, right. Well, it doesn't matter. We can't rely on the ploughs. When the wind stops and the snow isn't drifting anymore, I might be able to get down the road far enough to get help."

"How? The cars are stuck and it would take hours just to shovel a few feet. There's no snowmobile."

"No," agreed Will. "But when we were in the cellar, I noticed an old pair of cross country skis. I could give them a try to go for help."

"It's silly to be lying here carrying on a conversation," said Jennifer. "Let's all get up and have some coffee. We're not going to sleep anyhow. I'll see if we can make some sandwiches or something. I think there's some lasagna left over. We could warm it up."

She struggled to her feet and the others followed.

"Oh goodie, a picnic," said Marci. "What fun."

"Shut up, Marci," growled Jennifer, "Do you have any better ideas of how to pass the time? We just need to do something to get through the night."

"As long as no one suggests board games, I'm up for the midnight lunch," said Marci.

They all straggled around the kitchen getting in each other's way, no one really sure of what they were supposed to be doing. Sally noticed again that Jennifer's hand kept seeking her pocket as though she were fiddling with something in there.

She decided to come right out and ask. After all, waiting to discover a murderer or perhaps get caught by one with your closest group of friends, should surely pave the way for an honest question. She took a deep breath and said, "Jennifer. It's time you leveled with us. I know you had an ulterior motive for asking us here at this particular time. I think, considering the circumstances, you owe us an explanation."

Jennifer turned to face her, mouth open, Sally was sure, ready to give a resounding denial. Instead, she said. "Everyone sit down. I might as well tell you."

They sat on the makeshift beds, sitting in a semi-circle facing Jennifer. Sally wished she'd waited until she had a cup of coffee in her grasp. She felt as though she had nothing to do with her hands, but why should she be nervous? She wasn't the one on trial here.

"This doesn't concern you, Will," Jennifer began.

He snorted. "If you think I'm budging from this spot,

you're sadly mistaken. You owe me too."

She only hesitated a minute, then shrugged and began, "It's all because of what happened at that party before Halloween, the one in our final year."

They'd been to so many parties, Sally felt confused until it hit her. "Of course, Laura."

"Laura." Jennifer's voice spoke the name softly.

Sally could see Will's questioning look, but wisely, he didn't ask. Marci, she could tell, was going over the night in her mind. Sally could see the events as though through an old newsreel, the kind they used to run before a movie.

"It wasn't our fault," said Marci in a defensive tone. "It was Michael who gave her the pill. She was silly enough to take it. And who could tell the reaction she'd have to it. Sophie took one too, remember? She didn't go off the deep end."

"It probably wasn't Sophie's first time to try that particular form of self-medication," said Jennifer. "After all, Michael was known to deal a little bit of everything and Sophie had been keeping company with him for ages."

Sally smiled a little at the expression "keeping company." It was an old fashioned term she wouldn't associate with Sophie or Michael.

Laura, maybe, but not Sophie.

Jennifer gave her a sharp look and went on. "We should have stopped her. She was like a lamb to the slaughter. And, at the very least, we should have stayed with her to make sure she handled it all right. Instead, we all went home and left her there."

"Michael stayed," said Marci. "Even when Sophie came with us."

"Hmmph," said Jennifer. "I'm sure he wouldn't be much help to someone like Laura."

"And Nelson was there. He looked like he was about to make a play for Laura. He should have kept an eye on her."

Jennifer shivered slightly at the mention of Nelson's name. Sally didn't miss the movement and realized that was the root of Jennifer's guilt. She'd been lusting after Nelson all term, Sally remembered. That night, instead of devoting himself to Jennifer as she planned, he'd come on to Laura. Jennifer must have been beating herself up all these years, thinking she'd not stopped Laura because of a petty jealousy. Could they have stopped her? Sally wondered. She didn't think so. It happened so fast and Laura just gulped it down. It was afterwards they should have been there for her.

"We still should have helped her, stopped her from leaving on her own. We just left her there with a bunch of strangers who didn't care a fig what was going on."

Jennifer shook her head as though to chase away the image, and stood, saying, "Coffee's ready. Let's get something to eat."

"Aren't you going to tell us the rest of the story?" asked Marci. "How did that party twenty-five years ago and Laura's going into the river afterwards make you want this reunion?"

Jennifer didn't answer for a few minutes. Instead, they poured coffee and made their own snacks, carrying plates over one at a time to their impromptu campfire.

Finally, Jennifer spoke. "I met a man," she said.

"Who?" asked Marci.

"What does that have to do with Laura?" added Sally.

Will just concentrated on pushing the two thick slabs of bread with turkey cold cuts into his mouth, wiping his hand on his jeans as a spot of mustard exited the man-sized lunch.

"His name is Aaron Somers. He's Laura's brother."

Sally and Marci stared at her with identical expressions of disbelief, mouths hanging open.

"How did you meet him?" asked Marci. "Not that it matters."

"I met him when I sold him a piece of real estate. We hit it off and began seeing each other. Last week, he asked me to marry him. I said yes."

Sally looked at Jennifer's bare finger and said, "That's what's in your pocket. You've been fiddling with your engagement ring all night."

Jennifer gave a wry smile in answer. "I was waiting for the right time to tell you," she said. "And it never came."

"Does Aaron know that you knew Laura?" asked Sally. No wonder Jennifer was feeling lashings of guilt. She was one of the last people who could have stopped Laura, who could have saved her life.

"No, and that's why I wanted us to get together. Aaron

must never know. No one from all those years ago would remember who was at the party and, if they did, wouldn't give any significance to our talking to Laura. They might remember Michael if they remembered anyone. I think he got charged with possession shortly afterwards, but no one found anything on him that night."

Marci and Sally looked at each other. This was a change. Jennifer was usually the holder of secrets. Sally felt one moment of jubilation over the fact that they had her over a barrel until she thought more deeply about the reason. "Neither of us would tell him." She looked inquiringly at Marci, who nodded.

"Mum's the word," she said. "But if he ever does find out..." She left the sentence dangling.

"Well, he never will," said Jennifer. She took the ring out of her pocket then and put it on her finger. She held up her hand and examined it with a smirk of satisfaction. Sally wondered how deep her sense of guilt really went, or if her main fear was of discovery, not penance.

"Well," Marci said. "Now that that's out of the way, can we get on to the business at hand?"

"What business?" Jennifer yanked her hand down to her side.

"Have you forgotten that two of us are lying in a room down the hall, not breathing? And that we don't know who did it? And that whoever it is could be coming after the rest of us?" asked Marci, scowling at the others.

"No," said Jennifer. "But, short of keeping vigilance, I don't see what we can do until the authorities get here tomorrow, or whenever we can get a hold of them."

"Aren't you concerned that one of us is a killer?" asked Sally, wondering at Jennifer's aplomb. She always had the ability to appear in control, but this bordered on ridiculous. "I can't believe one of us did that to Sophie and Karen."

"And your alternative explanation?" said Marci. "No one else is in the house. No one else could possibly be outside in the storm. We've covered all this. It has to be one of us. Or are you so unconcerned because it's you?"

Sally nearly choked on her coffee. Will dropped a chunk out of his sandwich. Jennifer glared at Marci. It was one thing to speculate, but another to accuse outright.

"What reason would I have to kill either Sophie or Karen?"

"We all had secrets. You were the keeper of everyone's secrets," said Marci.

"That would give them a reason to want me out of the way. It wouldn't give me a motive for wanting to kill them. You have your reasoning a little backwards."

"We've just discovered you have secrets too. Maybe there was something you didn't want them to tell." Marci was persistent in her line of thought.

"Haven't you just been privy to my little secret? I was planning to tell you all later tonight and ask you all to keep mum around Aaron. Not that you'd run into him often anyway. If I'm willing to share with you, why wouldn't I have shared with them? We're friends, or at least I thought we were until you accused me of murder. And friends keep other friends' secrets."

"Okay, okay," said Marci. "I didn't really mean it. I know you could never murder anyone. I'm only frustrated because I can't think of anyone being a murderer. If you didn't do it, then who? Sally?" Marci screwed up her nose at the impossibility of the idea. "Me? I know I didn't do it, so who's left?"

Three pairs of eyes swung around to stare at Will.

"What?" he asked over a mouthful of turkey mayo. "I didn't even know you lot, except for when you came up in the summer and needed me to help with something. Why would I want to kill any of you? Look," he said, dusting the crumbs off his lap with two hands. Jennifer looked pointedly at their landfall on the floor, but said nothing. "We checked the cellar and no one was there. Let's check it again thoroughly and lay the idea of an outsider to rest. Then we can start questioning each other." He stood up. "First, we haul a piece of furniture over the cellar door. It opens out, so if we jam something against it, no one can come up from there."

They all jumped to attention. Doing something was always better than doing nothing. They pushed and pulled a heavy old sideboard across the room to bar the door to the cellar.

"Now I'm going to block the other entrance to the cellar—the outside one. It's set in enough that I can jam it with a couple of planks. There are some boards in the cellar. I'll get a hammer and some spikes and that will bar that door. If anyone is floating around out there, they won't be able to get in. Which means they'll freeze to death. While I'm there I'll clear everything out of that cupboard and look under the piles of blankets. I don't see how anyone could be in there without our seeing them, but we have to think of everything. You three stay here together. No one goes anywhere without the others, even to the bathroom, understood?"

They nodded. When Will had gone, they arranged themselves on the makeshift beds, sitting in a triangle, silently sipping coffee.

Jennifer was the first to speak. "That car you saw at the end of the road, Marci. Are you sure it was a Buick?"

"Of course I'm sure. I know my cars. My uncle used to have a dealership, remember? Aside from that it said Buick in nice silver letters. Why, what difference does it make?"

"None at all," said Jennifer.

"You wouldn't have asked if it wasn't important. Give. Who do you know with a blue Buick?"

As soon as the words were out of Marci's mouth, Sally could tell they were both thinking the same thing.

They turned to Jennifer, who was avoiding their eyes. "It's Aaron, isn't it? Aaron has a blue Buick."

Jennifer twisted her coffee cup around and then back before she answered. "Yes, he does. But it couldn't be his. He's gone to his daughter's house for the rest of the week. He doesn't even know how to find this cottage. And, anyhow, why would he want to hurt Sophie or Karen?"

"Think, Jennifer," said Sally. "Is there any way he could have found out about Laura and us and that night?"

"No! And if he did, he would have said something."

A look fluttered across her face that made Sally ask, "You just thought of something, Jennifer. What is it?"

"It's nothing really, but the night before I left... Well, I went to take a shower and when I came out, I thought something about him was different."

"And you never thought to tell us all this?" said Marci, her voice dripping with outrage.

"I thought he was cross because I was going. He tried to talk me out of it earlier."

"What could have happened while you were in the shower to make him change? Did the phone ring? Someone come to the door? Did you have something on your computer? What?"

Sally had a thought. "That night," she said. "Nelson brought that Polaroid camera, remember?"

Jennifer shuddered. "I remember everything about that night. I haven't been able to forget about it for twenty-five years."

"What happened to that picture? You took it home, didn't you?"

"Yes. I had it sitting in the flap of an old photo album. But it wasn't pasted into the pages. It was hidden away underneath some old play programs and things in the back page." Her voice slowed. "The album was in my desk drawer. But Aaron was never a curious sort. I can't see him rummaging around in my desk."

"Maybe he was looking for the address or wanted to know about the rest of us. We were all in the picture," Sally said.

"I wrote our names on the back and the date."

"It has to be Aaron," said Jennifer in wonder. "But Aaron wouldn't hurt us. He's not violent."

"But Aaron idolized his baby sister. Laura talked about him nonstop. Their parents were dead and he was father, mother, and brother all rolled up into one. Remember reading the newspaper articles about the family after it happened? He gave an interview."

"She's right," said Sally. "It's Aaron out there and it's payback. He's getting even with us for killing Laura."

"We didn't kill Laura," said Jennifer in a near shout. "We weren't responsible for what happened."

"But we didn't do anything to stop it, and maybe in Aaron's eyes, it's the same thing."

Marci said, "Of all the men you could have picked to have an affair with, why would you pick Aaron?"

"Listen," said Jennifer.

"Listen to what? I don't hear anything." Marci and Sally froze into listening mode.

"That's what I mean. Will should be hammering at the door, blocking it off. Or throwing things around searching."

All three jumped and ran to the front door. "Slide something across it," shouted Jennifer. "Block it like the cellar door." They began to slide the table towards the entrance.

Just as they reached the front door, it flew open. A tall, broad-shouldered man, with frost rimmed eyebrows giving him the appearance of an abominable snowman, stood there. Before she could move, he had circled Jennifer's neck with his arm. His other hand held a gun, a small handgun but lethal-looking all the same.

He pulled her into the room, using his foot to push the door shut behind him.

"Not a move out of either of you," he said. "One twitch by anyone and I'll shoot the one who moves first."

Marci and Sally slid slowly back in the direction he indicated towards the couches in front of the fire.

"Aaron, you're making a mistake. Things didn't happen the way you think."

"Shut up," he said. "I don't believe a word you say, ever again."

He let his arm loosen around Jennifer's neck, keeping the gun close to her head. With the arm he had just freed, he pulled lengths of rope from his coat pocket. He threw them onto the couch and spoke to Marci. "You tie her hands behind her back." He nodded towards Sally. "And do a good job. I'll be checking." His arm went back to encircle Jennifer in a tight hold.

When Marci had done the job and Aaron had inspected it, jerking on the rope to test its strength sharply enough to draw a gasp from Sally, he motioned for her to sit on the couch.

He let Jennifer free and instructed her to do the same with Marci. Then he made a one-handed loop in the final length of rope and, ordering Jennifer to hold her hands behind her, lassoed her hands with the rope. Only then did he set down the gun, still within reach as he completed the task of tying Jennifer.

They sat in a row on the couch; he sat on the one facing them, gun in his hand.

"Now I'm going to tell you why you're going to die," he said. "Isn't that nice of me? The other two didn't get that consideration. But I had to get the odds lower before I finished with the rest of you."

Chapter Seventeen

Sally listened to Aaron's apologia with the fascination of a witness to a snake charming. The initial shock of Aaron's thrust through the door had been replaced by a cold fear.

Of all the things she could be held accountable for in her life, why was this one going to be her undoing? The night of Laura's death had always been in the back of her mind, but had taken the back seat to other more indelible memories.

For a woman who had always found it imperative to accept the blame for every wrong thing in life, she had felt a strange lack of guilt over this one. She had spent a week agonizing over the unnecessary loss of a young life and then placed the blame squarely on the shoulders of Michael for supplying her with something he should have known she couldn't handle. Why had he done it? Not for payment since he had given it to her. Maybe to gain a new customer? Maybe for amusement to watch how a novice handled it? Sally saved a little of the guilt for Jennifer. She remembered her preoccupation with Nelson and the annoyance over his attraction to Laura. Gradually, Sally had shifted the blame further and further onto Jennifer. A way of coping, perhaps, with her resentment towards her over the years for being privy to her other unforgiveable crime.

She pulled at her wrists, but knew there was no hope of ever loosening the cords. Still, she had to try. It might help to drown out the stream of accusations that poured from Aaron. She sat as still as possible, slumped against the soft backing of the couch, twisting as well as she could while trying to keep her shoulders still.

"How could you ever think I could come to love the woman who killed my sister? You took the one bright thing out of my life as though she had no worth. And why? You shepherded the rest of your little group around. Why couldn't you have watched out for Laura? She used to talk about you, you know. She thought you were Joan of Arc and Madame Curie all rolled into one. She wanted to be part of your little club."

"I didn't know..." began Jennifer.

"Shut up! I don't want to hear anything from you. You are a liar and a coward and a murderer."

Jennifer paled and swung her glance away. Sally saw panic in her face that mirrored her own. This reunion was going to be their last.

"We didn't give her the pill." Marci ventured against his wrath.

"Do you think I don't know that? Your friend's lover gave it to her. I always knew that. But he's no longer with us. Did you miss him at your class homecomings? He died in a tragic accident the summer after Laura died." Aaron's anger disappeared momentarily under a sneer of contempt, and then swirled back. "He paid for his part in it and I thought it was over. That her killer had been judged and sentenced."

He stared at Jennifer so fiercely for a moment they wondered if he had finished his accusations. Sally braced herself for the roar of a gunshot.

But Aaron wasn't through. "Then I met you. I thought, what an opportunity to discover more about Laura's last days. You might be able to tell me things I didn't know and bring her back into my life in a way. I thought we could share memories of her." His voice choked and Sally thought the shimmer in his eye might not be only the gleam of hatred. He had unshed tears that threatened to spill over. Would that give them an opportunity? If his sight was diminished by the film of moisture, could they distract him, make a break for it? But how? Not with their hands behind their backs. They couldn't move quickly enough.

Sally thought about Mac. Would she ever see him again? Would she ever get the chance to beg his forgiveness? How could she have wasted the precious years with him eaten away with longing for what she couldn't have? An answering mist filled her own eyes.

"Stop snivelling." Aaron had swung the gun away from Jennifer to point directly at her. "You didn't waste any time crying for the life of my sister. And she was worth ten of you."

He switched his attention back to Jennifer. Sally's glance in trying to avoid Aaron's hate-filled stare landed on the basket beside her. On the little end table was a wicker container filled with decorations that Jennifer had scattered around the cottage to hold a little of the Christmas spirit into the week. Behind and nearly under the basket was a pair of scissors. A weapon! If she could reach them somehow and squirrel them away behind her back, maybe she could cut her ties.

Her glance must have lasted a second too long. Aaron turned his attention back to her. "Stop squirming," he said. "It will soon be over." And he smiled at her. A twitch of his lips and bared teeth that shot home to her just how far he had progressed into insanity. Nothing, no words, no last minute regrets, would sway him from his plans. She shrunk back into her seat and began to pray silently to the God that she wasn't sure existed.

Oh Mac. If I could only do it over again. I'd tell you everything and beg for your forgiveness.

Chapter Eighteen

Marci too had noted Sally's glance at the basket and, leaning back behind Sally, she could see what Aaron couldn't see from his angle—the scissors. But if Sally couldn't reach them, she certainly couldn't. She pulled at every angle she could think of to loosen her ropes. She thought of those wire puzzles with two items interlocked but with a trick twist you could pull them apart. How she wished she could do that to her bindings, but they were too tight. Where was Will? She knew the answer to that. If Aaron had been downstairs, he would have killed Will first. That's why they never heard him hammering.

Aaron wasn't done with his accusations. He seemed to be milking the last bit of revenge by watching their terror before he finished what he had come to do. "Then that night..." His jaw clenched and his hand tightened on the gun. What if he pulled the trigger without meaning to? What if he robbed them of their last few minutes of life? "You went to take a shower and I decided to look through your albums to see what I could find out about the others in your little clique. I actually pictured us all as friends, reminiscing about college days and about the part Laura had taken in all your lives." He gave a staccato bitter bark of a laugh. "How gullible could I be?"

Marci tried to drown out his voice, that terrible, monotonous, accusing voice. She thought of Dena—Dena whom she'd never see again. Why hadn't she told her how she felt? If by any miracle they managed to survive this, she would ask her to marry her, to declare their love in a ceremony. She didn't know why she had worried about Dena, why she had felt uncertainty. She was positive Dena loved her. There was no gamble in asking.

Another look at Aaron's face told her she'd probably never get the chance. They were all going to die.

Chapter Nineteen

Jennifer locked onto Aaron's gaze and flinched at the intensity of his hatred. She knew she had to look away. To hold his gaze meant a connection—a connection of accusation and guilt. How stupid could she have been, first to keep that old photo, and then to think she could build a relationship with the brother of the girl she—no, she wouldn't say "let die." It wasn't her fault. It wasn't.

"I memorized everything about your friends before I came. The first one, Sophie, she was so out of this world she didn't even know what she had done. It was her boyfriend who gave Laura the drug, but I didn't blame her as much as the rest of you. You all were aware. You could have stopped her." His gun hand jumped with each proclamation and Jennifer couldn't stop staring at the weapon. Would she see the bullet leave the barrel and come for her? No, it would be too fast.

"I was going to be all set up before you arrived. But then, I got lost in the storm and you were already here by the time I found you. Then my car skidded into the ditch. I thought for a minute I might have to just march in and shoot you, but I knew I had to make the others pay as well. So I hid in the cellar. I found the outside door unlocked—careless of you, and I used the big cupboard with the blankets to hide in. Then when that lackey of yours came looking for things, I piled them on top of me so I only made the pile of blankets look bigger. No one would think to look for a man under them. And I jammed the door. Then when he left, I slipped up the stairs and could hear everything you said through the door. When Sophie went out for her cigarette, I got her first. She never knew what hit her, but then she wasn't as guilty as the rest of you."

Jennifer played with her ropes like the others, but she had an advantage, she soon discovered. When Aaron tied her, he began with a single loop over her wrists and then bound her more tightly on top of the loop. If she could find the original loop amongst her bindings, maybe she could slip it over her wrist. She wished Aaron would focus on the others for a while. She couldn't move with any real effort while he stared at her. But even if she freed herself, then what? She couldn't launch herself across the space without Aaron shooting her before she even stood up. It wouldn't even save the others. They would still die. She thought about Will.

Aaron droned on. "I went back to the cellar. I knew I had to pick off at least two more of you. Six was too many to control with one gun, and even five might mean a danger that you wouldn't get to pay for your sins. Sins. That's a good one. Karen was a preacher's wife. Imagine that. I bet she never confessed her terrible sins to her husband. Finally, that man of yours came down again and I waited for him. I couldn't shoot him and warn you. So I caught him with the knife before he could see me. So I'm sorry if you were waiting for your knight in armor to come rescue you. He won't be coming."

Jennifer kept saying to herself, *Stupid, stupid,* as a sort of mantra. How could she have ever expected to keep her history with Laura away from Aaron? She should have realized his devotion to his sister was beyond normal with a fanatical edge to it.

She forced her attention back to the ropes that bound her. There! One had a little give to it. It must be the original. She worked at it, trying to free it from the others that covered it. She felt a little more give. Her heart sang with the thought of escape, but sobered when she followed through with—escape to where? But she kept on. Finally, she pushed and twisted and felt the loop slide off her wrist. She glanced at Aaron, trying to see him without making eye contact. Surely he would see the triumph in her eyes as she freed herself.

"Now," said Aaron. "Enough talk. You all know why you have to die. Who shall I start with?" He glared at Jennifer and said, "Not you. You get to be last. You get to watch your friends die for your cowardice and duplicity. You get to double-pay."

Jennifer massaged her wrist with her thumb behind her back and tried to think of some way she could get to Aaron before he sent the first bullet speeding towards one of them.

The front door shook and rattled. The wind? No. The wind had died. But the door rattled again, loudly, shaking with movement. Aaron swung to the door, gun pointed at the midsection. His attention diverted, Jennifer knew it was a slim chance but her only one. She jumped from her seat and flung herself across the few feet towards Aaron.

Startled, it only took him seconds to recover, but it was enough for Jennifer to throw him off balance as she reached for the gun. She couldn't get her hands on it, but it went off loudly as Jennifer and Aaron fell in a heap on the floor.

By now Marci and Sally had leapt from the couch and, wrists still bound, threw themselves into the fray. Marci planted one knee firmly on Aaron's wrist, pushing with all her might. Sally kneed the gun from his loosened grasp as Jennifer made a grab for it.

The door rattled again and opened an inch or two against the table they had tried to block it with. Jennifer held the gun in her shaking hands, aiming at Aaron.

"You'll never shoot," he said. "Not a coward like you." Jennifer wasn't sure either, but she kept a firm grip on the gun.

Marci now had the scissors in hand, cutting Sally's bindings. She turned so that Sally could do the same, but Sally jumped to the door, pulling it open.

As Jennifer's glance swung to Sally and the door, Aaron made a lunge for the gun. Jennifer held tight, squirming in his hold, twisting the gun to keep it under control. She felt her finger against the trigger and couldn't stop its movement as Aaron tugged at her arm. They swayed together in a macabre sort of dance, struggling for control of the gun. It went off with a muffled bang just as the door swung open.

Aaron and Jennifer hit the floor at the same time. Jennifer was half under Aaron, not sure which one of them had been shot as she watched the blood slide to the floor. She pulled herself out with a heave and saw Aaron's eyes flicker open and shut, his hand clutching his upper chest.

Trying to keep one eye on Aaron, she watched in amazement as Will fell to the floor inside the front door, also covered in blood, which seemed to trickle from his side where a knife lay lodged.

Sally reached for the knife. "No," said Marci. "It will only make him bleed more. Leave it." They grabbed blankets to cover Will. "He's still alive. He's breathing, but he's not responding. His eyes are closed. We have to do something."

Jennifer heard a movement behind her, distracted as she had been by Will's appearance. Aaron twisted slightly, trying to get his legs under him. "Help me first," said Jennifer. "Get some more of that rope. We have to restrain him."

They tied Aaron's hands, double checking to be sure the knots were tight, and then they bound his legs at the ankles as well to be sure he couldn't repeat what they had done.

Will's eyes flickered open briefly and closed again. "I don't think he's bleeding as much now," said Sally. "If we can keep him still, maybe he'll be all right until..."

"Until when? He's lost a lot of blood already. How long can he wait?"

Jennifer went to close the half open front door and said, "The worst is over. I don't think it's even snowing now and the wind has died down. Maybe soon, we can get out."

"We can't get Will and Aaron out without some sort of transport," said Marci. "We have to find a way to get help. Didn't Will say there was a set of skis downstairs? One of us could try to ski for help."

"You'd freeze to death," said Sally.

"But now we can see. We won't get lost. The white-out is over and the wind chill is down."

"Let's try the phones again," said Jennifer. "Try inside first and then a bit down the lane. If we keep trying, one of us might get a signal."

"Nothing yet," said Sally as she tried her cell. "Try the land line once more? Maybe they've been working on the lines."

Jennifer picked up the phone, expecting nothing. "I've got a dial tone," she said.

Chapter Twenty

Jennifer, Sally, and Marci sat huddled in the hospital, in a little waiting room apart from the main one. It seemed hours since the discovery of the magical dial tone.

Their frantic phone call had brought police on snowmobiles and, more importantly, a helicopter—an air ambulance that whisked Will and Aaron away. It had taken much longer for the three women to escape the questioning of the authorities. A photographer had taken scores of pictures, including some of their wrists where bruises showed they had been bound. Their story was a bizarre one, but surely they would be believed.

Sally knew that was only the beginning of their explanations. Even now, a constable sat at the end of the row of seats and she knew if one of them went to leave, she would spring to action.

As soon as they had called for help, Sally had phoned Mac, wanting his comfort, needing to hear his voice, but under the circumstances, she had to settle for a brief version of the events and an assurance she was all right. She knew he was here in the hospital, somewhere on the other side of the door, but being kept at bay until things were sorted to the satisfaction of the police.

They had each been given a quick once-over to be sure they needed no medical attention, and brought with no explanation to this little room to sit in silence waiting for news of Will. And Aaron, of course.

The phone on the constable's belt beeped and she picked it up, speaking into it quietly with her head averted. Sally couldn't make out a word.

Then the constable stood and beckoned to them with an almost smile. "Come with me," she said, leading them into the main corridor. She pulled aside, opening a door and motioned them in.

"Mac!" Sally flew into his arms, a jumble of words pouring out of her mouth that she knew made no sense, but she couldn't stop them.

"Ssshhh," he soothed as he held her tightly. "It's all right. I know. I know."

"But you don't know," she said. "You don't know."

"The police questioned us too," he said. "They asked what we knew about Aaron and his sister. About how she died." He stopped and pulled her apart from him to look directly at her, his expression so full of love and understanding Sally couldn't bear for him to know the worst. But she had to tell him.

They sat in two uncomfortable plastic chairs in the corner of the room. Sally could see Marci on the far side, deeply entrenched in the embrace of a golden-haired girl whose eyes were shimmering with tears as they met Sally's across Marci's shoulder. Jennifer was in an earnest conversation on her cell phone.

Sally brought her attention back to Mac. She had to tell him now before she lost her courage.

"None of this was your fault, Sally. None of you were to blame. Aaron is responsible for his actions, no one else." He gave a quick glance at Jennifer, but Sally could almost feel him biting his tongue.

"But back in college."

"Back in college wasn't your fault either. They told us how she died. How Aaron blamed you. He was just a tormented soul looking for answers, and when he couldn't find them, he had to blame someone." He hugged her again and said, "I think they'll let us go soon, but you'll want to know how Will is before we leave."

She nodded. "But that's not everything. You still don't know everything. All these years," she said. "All these years of wanting to have a baby."

She couldn't look directly at him. Sally needed to confess, but she couldn't stand to see the hurt in his eyes when she told him, so she confessed to the piece of worn tile on the floor in front of her chair.

"I did something unforgiveable in college," she said. "I

got pregnant and had an abortion. I'm sure that's why I can't get pregnant now. I had an infection and it must have spoiled me somehow. I'm so sorry, Mac. I married you under false impressions. I'm damaged goods."

She dared to look up and meet his eyes. She searched for censure, for recrimination, and all she saw was love.

"I know," he said. "I've always known."

"You knew? But how?"

"When we first married, you used to talk in your sleep. I put two and two together from some of the things you said."

"Why didn't you tell me you knew?" She felt a stirring of anger then. If Mac had told her he knew all along, she might not have felt so much guilt all these years.

He looked a little sheepish. "To begin, I wasn't sure. I only guessed. You were speaking gibberish some of the time. Then you didn't want to talk about it, so I thought you'd tell me when you were ready. It seemed you never were and, as time went on, it sort of became too late to say what I knew—or guessed."

"I'm so sorry, Mac. I'll never keep another secret from you as long as I live. If you forgive me for this one, that is."

"It was forgiven long ago, Sally. And I don't think any of you are as good at keeping secrets as you think you are."

The door opened and a figure in scrubs with a mask dangling around his chest walked in. He nodded to Jennifer.

"You're the cousin? Will Meadows' family?"

"Yes." Jennifer jumped to her feet.

The doctor's mouth twitched in a semi-smile and they knew before he spoke that Will would make it.

"He has a long road ahead," the doctor cautioned, "and some muscle damage may be permanent, but the good news is that he will live. I'm sorry, you can't see him for a while yet. The nurse will come and get you when you can visit. Even then, it will be a brief one." He turned and swung out of the room, not waiting for the sighs and smiles of relief that followed his announcement.

"I wonder about Aaron," Jennifer said. "I don't imagine anyone will come to let us know how he is."

But they did. Shortly after, the constable returned and told them they were free to go home but would be contacted the next day about interview times. There would be a lot more questions to answer.

"Aaron?" said Sally hesitantly, not really expecting an answer. "Did he make it?"

"Yes, he did. He's actually in better shape than your friend. But his story will likely be coming from a lawyer."

"Well she didn't tell us not to leave town, but I'm sure that was understood. You don't think Aaron will try to turn this on us, do you?" asked Marci.

"I think Aaron will be under the care of a psychiatrist when he testifies," said Mac. "I'm betting this will never go to trial. I don't think he'll deny anything he did because he feels it was justified. And now..." He stood up to emphasize his words. "I think we should all go home."

Sally wasn't quite ready to leave. "Karen's family," she said. "And Sophie's. What about them?"

"We'll find out tomorrow," said Mac with his hand on her arm. He led her out and Marci and Dena followed closely behind. Only Jennifer stood in the room unmoving, with her hand on her cell phone and a puzzled look on her face.

Sally knew it would be a long time before she could banish the fear she had felt staring at Aaron's trembling hand on the gun, and even longer to rid herself of the image of Aaron and Will bleeding on the cottage floor.

But even so, her heart felt lighter at the freedom of letting go of her past. She tucked her hand into the crook of her husband's elbow and smiled up at him.

"I think that's going to be my last reunion," she said. "Whatever Jennifer may plan."

About the Author

Sharon McGregor

Sharon McGregor is a west coast transplant from the Canadian prairies, on a mission to escape the cold. Her imagination and story weaving got its start when she was an only child living on a farm. She's moved on from cowgirl dreams to mystery and romance, but hasn't lost her love for horses. She writes humor, romance and cozies, sometimes a combination of all three.

When not writing or reading she is busy working in a shop she owns with her daughter, or walking the dogs along the ocean.

In spite of her attempts to escape winter, she loves watching her grandchildren at figure skating and hockey.

The main item not yet ticked on her bucket list is travel. She wants to set her foot on six continents-she'll give Antarctica a pass, thank you.